Deceive Me

Vi Carter

Contents

OTHER BOOKS BY VI CARTER

<u>THE BOYNE CLUB</u>
DARK #1
DARKER #2
DARKEST #3
PITCH BLACK #4

<u>THE OBSESSED DUET</u>
A DEADLY OBSESSION #1
A CRUEL CONFESSION #2

<u>THE CELLS OF KALASHOV</u>
THE SIXTH (NOVELLA)
THE COLLECTOR #1
THE HANDLER #2

<u>THE YOUNG IRISH REBELS</u>
MAFIA PRINCE #1
MAFIA KING #2
MAFIA GAMES #3
MAFIA BOSS #4

<u>BROKEN PEOPLE DUET</u>

DECEIVE ME #1
SAVE ME #2

WARNING

This book is a dark romance. It contains scenes that may trigger some readers and should be read by those only 18 or older.

BLURB

Jared

They say love and hate dance together along the same line.

My feelings for Layla don't dance on the line; they destroy it.

It's been seven years since she disappeared without a trace.

And now she's back, but things have changed—I've changed.

I'm no longer the Jared she remembers, the boy who wanted to protect her.

I'm very much my father's son, and I take what I want, and what I want is Layla.

But this time, I'm keeping her forever.

Layla

Seven years—that's how long it's been since I've seen him.

After painstakingly putting myself back together, I'm finally ready to start a life without his memory chasing my every step.

Imagine my surprise when my new beginning leads me straight back to him.

Only he's not the boy I remember.

He's angry.

Damaged.

Hiding secrets that want to destroy him.

He hates me. He wants me.

I'm not sure I'll survive the man he has become. His demons threaten to destroy us both.

Part One of the Broken People Duet

PROLOGUE

JARED

*P*OVERTY.

It's something I'm not accustomed to, not anymore. Not since my father took me from the slums and brought me to his billionaire mansion. He told me it was all mine and that I needed to buck up and be the son I was destined to be.

I don't think I can ever live up to his expectations.

The car slows as I approach Woodview Estate. It gives me the fucking shivers. I'm not afraid; it's more of an old memory, like a fire burning in my mind. One I extinguish as I park my new BMW along the curb. This place is devoid of life, not even the grass has survived. The wilted shrubbery hangs over the side of the curbing. This is Ireland, so it rains all the time, but this place is forsaken. Even the rain doesn't bother to piss on the landscape. As I stare around me and study a little closer, I start to notice signs of life.

In front of me is a large row of houses, and at the corner of the end house, shadows of movement catch my eye. Behind drawn curtains, light seeps through the small cracks. I'm sure some watch me from the windows. My presence here has not gone unnoticed. I get out of the car and lock the doors. Shadows creep closer. Most of the men have their faces camouflaged inside hoodies. I focus on house number six. I'm apprehensive of the guys at my back, circling closer to my car. The moment I push open the gate to number six, they murmur.

Their whispers reach my ears. "He's with Chester. We'd better scram."

Like rats, they scurry. Chester must be the man I'm seeking. Warren only gave me an address, no name. I knock on the door three times before someone answers. The guy who opens it isn't looking at me, so I'm faced with his profile. Tribal tats rise from the collar of his jersey and wrap around his neck.

He draws a drag of a cigarette, side-eyeing me. His hands are coated in tattoos too. "What do you want?"

"I'm looking for Chester."

This fucker is a wolf, but I'm no lamb. He faces me, flings the cigarette past my shoulder, and grins. "What for?"

"Can I come in?" I ask, and I take a step closer to him.

His grin transforms into a sneer, but he steps back. "Sure."

I don't like that he's at my back, but I continue to keep a relaxed posture as I walk into the dingy entrance. The smell of smoke and something stronger clings to everything.

"I didn't pick up what you wanted." He passes me while lighting up another cigarette. He shoulders a door to our left open, and we step into a sitting room that's full of guys who are sporting tats just like his. I unquestionably have the right house.

He plops down between two other men on the couch. All eyes are on me.

"I didn't say what I wanted." I point at the empty armchair to my left. The guy, who I assume is Chester, nods, and I sit down, opening my jacket.

R&B music plays in the background. A fog of smoke floats close to the ceiling.

A guy near me offers me a rolled-up cigarette. It doesn't smell like smoke, and I decline before facing Chester. "Could we talk somewhere private?"

He glances at the other men, who laugh, before he faces me. "No. If you have something to say, say it."

I'm not telling him shit in front of everyone. They all move when I reach into my pocket. I raise one hand as I slowly withdraw the envelope of cash with the other. "Three grand for a word in private, Chester."

He jerks his chin, and I toss the envelope to him. He catches the cash, shreds it open, and starts counting. Once he's satisfied, he passes the stash of cash to the guy beside him before standing.

"You've bought yourself five minutes."

My five minutes are in the entrance hall. I assumed it would be someplace more private, but I take the time I'm offered. "I need a gun."

"What makes you think I can get you one?"

"Warren O'Reagan gave me your address," I explain.

Something shifts in Chester's stance. "You don't look like a friend of Warren's."

I smirk. "Neither do you."

Chester jerks his chin again. "It will cost you."

"Name your price."

He thinks about it. "Ten grand."

For a fucking gun? "I want it wiped."

"It'll be untraceable. But it will take time."

"How long?"

He takes a drag of his cigarette before stepping to the front door. Opening it, he flicks the cigarette outside. He pauses before looking back at me. "Is that your car?"

"Yeah." I stride toward him.

He lets out a whistle. "Touch the car and you die." He issues the warning to the group outside and closes the door. "I should have asked for more money since you're driving a car like that." He grins.

I don't smile. "I'll give you five grand tomorrow and the other five grand when I have the gun."

He nods, and I hold out my hand. Chester hesitates before he grips my fingers. "We have a deal."

I'm ready to go when he asks a question he shouldn't. "What do you want it for?"

I glare at him. "I'll see you tomorrow."

"Just asking, brother. You know it won't end all your problems." He holds up his thumb and forefinger, mimicking a gun.

"It might end one," I say before I take off. My car is still unscathed. Driving out of the estate doesn't make the memories evaporate; instead, I'm yanked right back to my childhood. The very reason I want a gun.

Everything comes full circle. My father once said, "What's meant for you won't go by you. Justice will be served in this life or another."

I say, fuck that. If Justice isn't served the way it should be, then I'll take matters into my own hands and deliver my kind of justice.

Once I do this, my life will be my own again. I'll finally be able to live.

CHAPTER ONE

LAYLA

So MUCH CAN CHANGE in a moment; a lot can change in seven years. Seven years. That's how long it's been since I've seen Jared. Seven years to the day, when I was dragged from his arms kicking and screaming. He fought so hard to keep me with him. He fought to the point that his violence made me shiver.

The sound of the sliding door opening pulls me away from my thoughts. The swing bench creaks as Evelyn sits down. The smell of her moisturizer on her olive-tone arms consumes me. Glancing up from my hands, I find her deep brown eyes watching me. She brushes long locks of black hair over her shoulder before smiling at me softly. "You don't have to do this."

My heart skips a beat at how much I want to walk away from this, but I can't. I can't walk away, because Evelyn and Carl have packed up their lives and moved halfway across Ireland so I can go to the best college. I'm both nervous and excited at the prospect of starting over in a new place. This is my chance to start a new life and leave the past behind.

"Close your eyes and take a breath."

I do what Evelyn instructs.

"Tell me what you're thinking about." Evelyn speaks in her calming voice. She's a counselor. Some would say I'm lucky to have been adopted by her and Carl, but her voice of reason isn't always welcome. Right now, though, I need her.

"Jared." His name causes Evelyn to stiffen beside me. Her reaction to him always confuses me. She makes it seem as if Jared was the one who hurt me, when he was the one who protected me. I drop my hands to my lap before opening my eyes. "I was thinking about him. How he always protected me."

Evelyn takes my hand in hers. "Now it's my and Carl's turn to protect you." She brushes a loose strand of blonde hair behind my ear. I want to ask her why she gets uneasy when I talk about Jared, but I don't get the chance.

Carl steps out into the backyard with a steaming hot mug of coffee in his hands. His soft green eyes and olive skin make him attractive, even for his fifty years. He keeps himself in shape. "It's time to go." He shows us his watch. I can't read the front face from this distance, but I nod and hop up from the bench. Evelyn stands behind me, placing both her hands on my shoulders. The slight squeeze fills me with the strength I need. I inhale a deep breath and swallow. "I'm ready," I say to Carl.

The smile he gives me is stuffed to the gills with encouragement.

I have spent seven years in therapy trying to erase every slap and thump, every word and memory, and now it's all coming back. For some reason, starting over makes me go back to the start—to Bert and Ronnie. To Jared. Most times, I keep the knowledge to myself that I have never really let go of Jared. I keep that information bottled up.

I want to prove to Carl and Evelyn that they saved me—that they fixed me.

I gather my phone and bag, hurrying to the car before I change my mind. The click of it being unlocked has me climbing into the back. Evelyn and Carl both get in and glance at each other. They share a look for only a split second, and it has me sinking into the car seat. They don't think I'm strong enough.

"I'm ready," I say once again, even as my throat threatens to close. Pulling down the visor, Evelyn glances at me in the mirror with a soft smile that wrinkles the skin around her brown eyes. "We know you are, sweetheart."

Carl starts the car and backs out of the drive. My gaze drifts away from Evelyn's and to the neat rows of houses we pass. Each one is white, and each one is as perfect as the next. It's a far cry from where I came from. Bert's house was unkempt and dilapidated, a bit like its occupants.

"I could have driven," I say, staring out the window.

"We wanted to take you," Carl says. Silence filters in, and I'm waiting for someone to pierce the quietness. "If—and I'm only saying if, Layla—you change your mind, we can always turn back." The softness and kindness in his voice still startles me sometimes. Even after seven years of witnessing what a great man he is, I can't erase the other twelve.

My childhood in foster care was a different time and a different life, one that I dip into for a reference, but I never stay there. "Thanks, Carl. But I want to do this. I mean, it's only college." I force a wobbly smile.

Carl gazes at me in the rearview mirror; I catch my own reflection and look away. My white skin is ghostly.

Another glance is shared between Carl and Evelyn. I pretend I don't see it as I clutch my bag tighter. They are such good people, and I'm the only child they adopted, not being able to have children themselves. I often wonder why people who deserve to have children can't, and the ones who shouldn't be allowed to have children can. Is it God's plan, or is it just a flaw in the body? To me, it's such a shame. Both of them are amazing.

The drive to Kingscourt College feels like it takes forever. I've made this journey a few times in the car that Carl and Evelyn had purchased for my nineteenth birthday only two weeks ago. The red starlet was a lavish gift, but one they both said was nothing. It isn't new, but to me, it's perfect. The car will take me to school so I won't have to rely on Carl or Evelyn to drive me.

"I was thinking when we pick you up, we could stop and grab some Chinese," Evelyn says.

I tense as the large black iron gates loom in front of us. The castle that houses Kingscourt College is set deep in the background and grows larger as Carl continues to drive. I glance up at the monstrous structure where I will spend the next three years studying business.

"Yeah, that would be great." I swallow the enormous lump in my throat as we pull into the parking lot. Food is the furthest thing from my mind right now.

Carl knocks off the car, and I quickly grab the bottle of water out of my bag. After taking a nervous gulp, I replace the blue lid. *Stop delaying. You can do this.*

Repeating this in my head gives me the strength to climb out of the car. I hold on to the door and bend my head to look back in. Both Carl and Evelyn turn to look at me.

"I'm going to be fine," I remind them.

"You can get back into the car." Carl's words have my head dipping as my heart feels like it's shrinking.

"But we both know you're strong enough to do this." Evelyn's words wrestle a smile out of me as I look from her to Carl.

"You are." Carl smiles back, and I release the car door and close it. I don't look back as I drag my bag across my shoulder. Other students gather around vehicles parked across from Carl's car. They glance at me, but I'm dismissed quickly. I take a peek back at Evelyn and Carl, who are still sitting in the car watching me. I give them a little wave and walk across the vast open space that's half-filled with cars.

The grass softens my steps as I leave the parking lot, and I crane my neck back to really take in Kingscourt College. The gray stone of the castle tells a story of time. The closer I get, the more scars I see along the stone. I walk along the footpath and trail my fingers across the harsh ridges. History intrigues me. It's there for us to learn from. We never do, but it's there all the same. My fingers leave the wall as two guys walk past me. One smiles, and I try smiling back. His mouth tugs higher, telling me I'm doing great. I look back at the parking lot, wanting Carl and Evelyn to see my progress already, but Carl's Mercedes is gone.

I turn away and take the three steps up to the main red doors. One door is open, a black chock keeping it in place. The light inside the lobby is dim, and it takes my eyes a moment to adjust.

Chairs are placed all along the wall, where people sit waiting. Some appear dressed more for an interview rather than college. My eyes collide with a girl whose lips remain in a thin, straight line as she watches my progress down the hall. Her high blonde ponytail is something I could never achieve with my hair. My long blonde strands are too fine to stay in place. I tuck a strand behind my ear and approach a large reception desk.

The air in the lobby is heavy and warm, and I find myself pulling at the blouse that Evelyn laid out for me. I matched it with my favorite black skinny jeans and black boots. I ditched the suit jacket she had left for me—it made me appear too formal—but seeing how everyone else is dressed, I regret leaving it on my bed.

"Take a seat." The receptionist doesn't even look up as she speaks. When I don't scurry away, she sighs. "Take a seat." She looks at me from under her red-rimmed glasses, and I step away from the desk and turn to find the occupants of the chairs watching me.

The black plastic chair I sit on is warm. My gaze collides with the blonde girl, her eyes narrow, and I look away and sit in silence as other students filter into the lobby and make their way to their classes. My attention is drawn to the door every time I hear a creak. Each time, my heart leaps as more students filter in and others leave. The receptionist stands and points at the first seat. Time moves slowly. I keep taking peeks at the blonde girl, and she smirks. When she's called, she flicks her hair as she walks past me. She has the figure that most girls would die or starve for. She leans in on the desk, and the receptionist laughs.

When it's my turn, I gather my bag and approach the desk. The receptionist gives me a brief second of her attention before sliding her glasses up on her head. "How can I help?"

"HI, I'm Layla Masters. I'm new here. I'm looking for the gym." I attempt a smile.

She slides the glasses back down on her face. "Down the hall. On your left you will see a set of Brown double doors. You'd better go before you're late." Her words catch me off guard.

"Thank you." I leave the desk and follow her directions to the brown double doors. I take a final look at my attire before reaching for the handle. I didn't bring my sports uniform in hopes that I could sit this one out. Taking gym class isn't standard for Irish colleges, but Kingscourt has made this class mandatory.

I pull the door open to have every head turn in my direction. If that's not bad enough, I'm very aware that all the men wear shorts, and the girls are in skirts.

"Get changed and join us on the floor," the coach shouts.

"I don't have a uniform." My voice is low.

He shakes his head and walks closer to me. "There are some spare uniforms in the large green locker." The coach blows his whistle. "Hurry up. Let's start."

I want to say no, but the words get lodged in my throat. The blonde girl I saw earlier smirks before leaning into a guy beside her. A guy whose brown eyes are so deep they appear almost black. But, in those eyes, I see a young boy—one I've dreamt of for the last seven years.

Jared.

I've found Jared. I've found home.

CHAPTER TWO

LAYLA

D ISBELIEF WEIGHS SO HEAVILY on my heart that I'm looking for a sign that he isn't Jared. His eyes flash with a warning that is soaked with recognition before they flare up. The hate burns the light away, and I'm left staring at a stranger.

A girl's laughter draws my attention to the group, and they're watching me as I stare at Jared. The coach has his back to us as he gathers up a net of balls.

The blonde girl's laughter dies, and she steps closer to Jared. He doesn't seem to notice the motion as he narrows his gaze, and his jaw tightens.

"What are you looking at?"

Oh God, his voice...

The tone is deeper, but I know that voice. The hairs rise on the back of my neck as I continue to stare at his broad chest. I try to comprehend his question, which is stuffed to the gills with bitterness.

The blonde clears her throat, and her small hand brushes against Jared's shoulder. He noticeably tenses under her touch, but I see what she's doing. She's claiming him.

I can't breathe.

My mind can't accept what I'm seeing—his face, a face I looked at every day. One I loved seeing. One I feared I would never see again. Yet here he is, against all odds. His features are the same, but stronger and manly. He's harshly beautiful.

My bag slips off my shoulder, and I can't stop the motion as it hits the ground. This can't be real. His jaw is stronger, his dark eyes deeper, his lips fuller. He's so much bigger, so much angrier. But this is Jared.

I always knew that when he grew up, he would be something amazing to look at. I was right.

My heart tries to burst from my chest as his lip curls into a sneer like the edges of burning paper. I'm trying to stay still as he drags his gaze across my body, even as my skin feels like it's on fire.

He doesn't recognize me.

He steps forward, detangling himself from the girl, and slowly starts walking toward me. The rise and fall of his shoulders remind me of a lion. I should run. I hold still, reminding myself that I have nothing to fear from him.

"I asked you a question. What are you looking at?" The cruel sneer remains on his fiercely handsome face. The closer he comes, the more my certainty of who he is wavers. He's so much bigger than I am. His width seems to block out the world behind him, and it's like a dark veil falls over me.

"Jared." I say his name as my throat burns.

His jaw tightens, pain twists his features, and soon it's all swallowed with a hate I don't understand.

"Ms. Masters, why are you still standing here?"

The world snaps back into focus. The coach approaches me.

"Get changed now," he barks, and he blows his whistle, which pierces the space. "Everyone, let's go." He claps his hands, and Jared jogs backward away from me. He spins when he reaches his group of friends, who all glare at me.

"Ms. Masters!" The shout from the coach has the heat across my cheeks flaring up as I gather my bag off the floor and turn to find a door with a sign for the locker rooms above it.

I'm trying to get my breathing under control as I open the green locker to find a stack of sport uniforms. I don't find my size until I'm halfway down the pile. I take off my shirt and slip on the baby blue T-shirt.

The longer I'm away from Jared, the more I question if that's really him. If that's really the boy who protected me and saved me. My stomach twists, and my hands tighten on the gray skirt. I take a few more deep breaths and strip off my trousers to put on the skirt. My scarred leg has me sitting on the cold bench as a memory assaults me.

I take tiny baby steps, clutching the pink plastic basin in my hands. The sudsy water splashes from side to side, threatening to spill over. When I reach Bert, I'm proud that I haven't spilled a drop. After placing the basin to my left, I take the towel off my shoulder and spread it between Bert's feet. His laces are always covered in dust and dirt from his workdays in construction. Pulling off his large size-twelve boots nearly sends me falling back, but I keep my balance.

I take off his sweaty, smelly socks on autopilot. He stretches his toes like a cat stretching itself while I put the basin in its place. Bert rolls up his jeans to his knees. I don't move. I wait until his feet are in the basin. He dips his toes, barely breaking the surface of the water. Bert lifts his legs quickly, his eyes growing round and wide. My heart stills.

"You tried to burn me," Bert accuses.

I shake my head in denial, unable to speak, and he plants his feet on either side of the basin. I fall back at his sudden movement.

"You little bitch."

I shake my head again, words refusing to come to me.

Scrambling back, I try to avoid the flying basin as Bert kicks it in a rage. Water sloshes across my legs and onto the wooden floor. I cower, trying to disappear as the basin collides with my side. Keeping my eyes closed tightly, I tuck my head into my chest as my heart beats wildly. The ground disappears beneath me, and I'm airborne. My back roars at the abuse as Bert smashes me against the wall. His large hand encircles my throat, and my small feet dangle near his knees. I claw at his hands, terrified for the first time that I might die. It isn't just his grip around my throat, but the violence in his eyes. My nails sink into his large hands, which tighten at a neck-breaking strength.

I kick and claw as light and strength start to disappear.

As Jared pounds his fists into Bert's head, trying to make him release me, I still can't breathe. Bert's grip leaves my throat, and I hit the ground; the impact sends pain into my hip, but it's nothing like the pain in my throat.

Jared.

I get up off the bench and finish getting ready. I take a pair of gray sneakers that are too big and slip them on. I'm searching for a moment in the mirror where I tell myself how strong I am and that I've got this, but words cower deep in my belly, just like always.

"Ms. Masters, do you need assistance?" a voice calls in.

I scurry away from the mirror, and as I leave the locker room, I meet the coach, who hands me a ball. Everyone is passing them back and forth to each other.

"Alex, you're with Layla."

My fingers tighten around the ball. Alex, the blonde girl, approaches with disdain, twisting her pretty features. Her focus drops to my leg, and she tilts her head to the side. False pity fills her eyes.

"I'm sure the coach would let you wear sweatpants, considering..." She flicks her hair.

Once again, words fail me, and I try to catch Jared's eye, but he's further down, engrossed in passing a ball. He doesn't remember me. His right hand has a dark ink band around the wrist. I think it's a tattoo, but I can't be sure from this distance.

Fingers click in front of my face. "I'd like to get some physical activity done today." She follows my line of sight before a hateful laugh falls from her ruby red lips. "So out of your league. Jay wouldn't give you a second glance."

I fire the ball at Alex, and she catches it quickly.

"Jay?"

Her expression hardens. "That's what I said."

She passes the ball to me, and we continue this as the knowledge that this guy isn't Jared slowly sinks in. He may remind me of Jared, but from his hostile glares, I can assume that the recognition I thought I saw isn't really there. He has no idea who I am.

When class ends, I'm a little less shaky and quickly change back into my clothes. Alex and two other girls talk openly about me gawking at Jay. When their words grow hushed, I hear them talking about my scarred leg.

I leave without looking at the circle of mean girls. That's what they are, mean girls. Most schools have them, but I didn't expect to find the mean girls in college. I've been fortunate enough not to attract the attention of them before. I've always been able to fly under the radar.

Passing through the gym, I can't help but search for Jay. The area is empty.

Taking out my schedule, I check to see what my next class is. Pivoting, I stop as I come face-to-face with a girl who wears a name tag: Ashley. Her tawny skin is flawless, as is her long black ponytail. With eyes not quite green or brown focused on me intently, I shuffle my feet, feeling self-aware. What does she see when she looks at me?

A tall, thin, and pale girl who is staring at her for far too long?

"I've been assigned to be your guide." Her accent sounds Hispanic, which makes sense with her features. She turns on her heel with a slight smile. Her movements remind me of a ballerina. Her frame isn't really suited to that, though, as she's all curves. "By the way, I'm Ashley." She pulls at her name tag as she speaks. "I'll show you where we eat."

I follow Ashley to a large empty room that is lined with benches and long tables. Right now, the space is empty, but I can imagine the activity during break times. This is one space I will avoid. Two ladies dressed in white aprons hustle behind a long silver steam table.

"Great," I say.

Ashley grins, flashing white teeth. "It's not a restaurant, but the food is decent. Trust me, after morning classes, this place is like a haven."

I nod. *Not to me.*

Being around people isn't something I do often, unless you count Morgan, the girl who lives across the street from me. We moved here only two weeks ago and her mother greeted us on our first day in the neighbored. That night I ended up going out with Morgan and her friends just to please Carl and Evelyn.

I follow her out to the bustling hallway. She points a lot as she tells me where everything is. "That's the library. Avoid the back area." She rolls her eyes as she glances at me over her shoulder. "That's where people go for fun times."

I'm making notes. *Avoid the library and the lunch area.* We stop at a gray door.

"So this is our business class. We better go in before we're late." She pushes open the door, and we step into the lecture room. I don't look around me. I keep focused on the steps I climb until I see a row at the back empty. That's where I sit, with my single notepad and pen. Coming to a new college halfway through the year is tougher than I imagined. This college is way ahead of where I left off at my old college. I spend the next few hours going from one class to the next. Ashley never leaves me, and I'm grateful for her constant chatter.

"So, it's lunch now. Are you good at finding your way there?"

My blood heats up in my veins at the thought of being left on my own, but I need to rely on myself. I nod. "Yeah, sure, I'm good."

The heat spreads across my checks, but Ashley doesn't seem to notice as she rolls her shoulders before heading toward the mass of students. I look around and decide to make my way outside. I'm tempted to glance up and make eye contact with people, but after my run-in with who I thought was Jared, my nerves are rattled, and my stamina has dwindled to nothing.

A group of guys have gathered close to the main door blocking me from leaving.

The scent of cigarette smoke surrounds them. All of them have similar features to Ashley's. My steps falter at the sight of the group, but I push one leg in front of the other until I reach the door..

One of the guys, who wears jeans that hang way too low and a T-shirt that could house a few guys his size, grins at me. His eyes travel from my flat black shoes, up to my black jeans, and on to my white shirt.

"You're new?" he says with a wide smirk.

"Yes. I just started today." I'm ready to walk away when he steps in front of me. "Can I help you with something?" I ask, slinging my bag over my shoulder.

"You can help me with a few things."

The suggestive remark has his friend laughing while bumping into him. "Man, you hittin' on whitey?"

I can feel each nerve zing inside of me. I want to run out of the building. I force a smile and sidestep them. My hands roll into fists until my knuckles turn white and my heart hammers.

Don't run.

"Lucas, you dumb..." Ashley gives me a quick look before glancing back at the trio. The one who spoke to me is Lucas.

"What are you doing?" Her hands go to her hips, and she looks fierce. I want to be like her when I grow up.

"Don't be like that, *hermana,*" Lucas says.

Ashley tuts at his words. "Does *Madre* know you're here, *bobo?*"

The other boy snickers. "She called you a fool!"

"You are a *bobo* too, Sam," Ashley says.

Sam's smile melts off his face.

"We are only messing, Ashley. Relax," Lucas says, removing a pack of cigarettes and a lighter from his pocket.

Ashley moves away from Lucas and Sam, who split and go back down the main corridor, but not before calling goodbye to Ashley and blowing her kisses—ones she doesn't respond to.

As they leave, a familiar voice rises up.

Why didn't I say something?

How many times have I frozen in the past? When Bert was screaming a question at me, I'd freeze. Not responding was the worst thing to do, but I always *froze.*

I am such an idiot.

"Are you okay, Layla?"

My head jerks up at Ashley's voice. "Yeah, fine. Why?"

Ashley looks away from me briefly, then her nose scrunches up as she speaks. "You've been staring at the same spot for the last few minutes."

The heat comes again, fast and hard—my face blazes.

"Look, I know Lucas and Sam can be full-on. But they're harmless." Ashley tucks her hands into her shirt pockets while leaning against the wall. Her stance looks so relaxed, but her eyes once again are fierce, making them grow more brown than green.

"I'm just... not good with new people."

She nods like she gets it, but there's no way she could understand what I'm saying, and I'm not going to enlighten her about my childhood from hell.

"Lucas and Sam are my brothers, and they wouldn't hurt a fly. They're Idiots, but they wouldn't hurt anyone." Ashley stands straight with a goofy grin on her face. "Do you have any brothers or sisters?"

It's a simple question that people ask each other all the time. For me, it's one of the hardest. My nerves are frazzled, and I push back on my heels. If I say I do, she'll ask more questions. If I say I don't, I feel like I'm hiding Jared, Riley, and Nelson. My throat dries up and my pulse spikes. "Oh. I better get going. I forgot my purse." She turns away while nodding. "We'll chat later."

I try to mirror her smile. "Yeah. Great."

The moment Ashley is gone, I grip my bag and walkout of the building.

Tomorrow will be better. First days are always the worst. I'll try harder. I won't search for Jared in every set of brown eyes.

My nose and throat burn as I take a peek at the car park. Carl won't be here yet, and it gives me a few moments to pull myself together. I don't get to process much more, as a large hand springs out, and I'm dragged around the side of the building. The moment my back hits the wall, I'm frozen under the heavy stare of a set of dark, angry eyes.

And I'm at it again. All I can think about is Jared.

CHAPTER THREE

JARED

MY HANDS DEMAND I hurt her. I push harder on her small shoulders, and the foolish boy in me screams to take my hands off what's his. What he has spent years searching for, each time coming up emptier and a little angrier than the last. Yet, here she is, staring up at me with wide blue eyes. Her scent seems to envelop me, and I dig a little deeper into her shoulders.

I could snap her so easily. I want to.

She shouldn't be here.

"What the fuck do you want?" I bark and lean in, inhaling her aromatic lavender scent.

Layla.

Anger bubbles through me, and my back arches.

"You're the one who dragged me over here." Her voice is stronger, her gaze more defiant than she displayed in the gym. Earlier, she looked like a victim. I remember how good she always was at playing the victim.

I grin and take some of the pressure off her shoulders but don't remove my hands completely. "Because you were staring at me like some lovesick puppy." I say each word with a mocking tone.

Her lip trembles, and my gaze lingers on her mouth. She's still Layla, just older. More womanly. That fact isn't lost on me, with all the curves she displayed in gym class. She isn't someone who fades into the background. She always stood out, even when she didn't want to. I don't need her to be here. I don't need the distraction.

"I thought you were someone else, but I was wrong."

I release her, and she reaches up and rubs her shoulders. I don't step back. I don't want to walk away from her. The pull that was always there hasn't eased with time. If anything, it seems stronger.

I hate her.

"Let's hope your drooling over me ends." I fold my arms across my chest. I know my size will intimidate her. I battle with the need to protect her. It's all I knew. All I cared about. She was the reason I got up, the reason I lived. The reason I fought to survive. Until she left, not giving a fucking care in the world about me.

"I thought you were someone else," she says again. Pain drags down her lips.

Fuck her.

"I don't want your sob story." I lean in close to her and dip my head so that she can hear me very clearly. "Stay out of my way, Layla, or I'll make sure you regret ever crossing my path."

Her chest rises and falls faster. My words fully sink in; I've made my point. Her swanlike neck draws my hand to it. She inhales sharply as I tighten my fingers around her fragile throat. Her pale skin is soft. I can imagine pressing kisses along the flesh. I tighten my fingers further, trying to banish the thought.

She pulls away. "Get your hands off me." Her hysteria pierces my anger. The protective boy in me has me removing my hand, and yet I can't step away from her.

She ducks under my arm and flees while I stare at the wall, wondering what the fuck is wrong with me.

I tighten my hand into a fist, and all I want to do is smash it into the wall.

"What was that about?" Alex's voice springs up behind me.

I loosen my fists, and I turn to her wearing my signature *I don't give a fuck* smirk. "I have that effect on women. They throw themselves at me. I was just telling her I wasn't interested."

Alex assesses me for a moment. "It looked a little intense."

I step closer to Alex and let my smirk manifest into a smile. "I'm an intense guy."

Her posture relaxes before her lips tug up. "I can verify that is true, Jay." She winks at me.

I start walking toward the parking lot while looking for a blonde girl who shouldn't be here. Did she search for me over the years too? It really doesn't matter. I want to stay focused, and she's too great of a distraction.

"So, this charity event tonight..." I start.

I glance at Alex, and she rolls her eyes dramatically. "Do you have to go too?"

"Yes. Raising money for starving kids while we eat a seven-course meal and drink our fill seems like such a fitting thing to do." Sarcasm drips from my words.

"You seem bothered." Her words hold an accusation.

I drag back my control that Layla rattled. The last person I want to see a crack in my armor is Alex. She's clever, and she would do anything to climb higher in our social circles. That includes handing me to the wolves if need be. I stop walking. "Maybe I am bothered." I lean into her.

She smiles. "Bothered and intense. I do like that combination."

Alex is striking. Her reasons for liking me are far more calculating than any physical attraction. She knows our parents want us together. We would be a powerhouse. I've tasted her strawberry-flavored lips many times before, and I'd happily taste them again.

"I'll see you tonight," I say once I reach my vehicle. I glance around the parking lot, but I don't see Layla.

"I look forward to it." Alex still lingers at my car as I climb in.

I close the door and lose my smile. She's still watching me as I reverse out of the parking spot.

***

"Jay, today is not the day," Rex shouts as he climbs out of the ring. He's sweaty from training some new guy who waves at me like he knows me. For Rex's sake, I wave back.

"I need to blow off some steam." I remove my sweater and throw it alongside the ring.

"I'm training someone." Rex juts his chin over his shoulder. The new guy is watching us.

"Does he bring in as much money as I do?" I ask as I pick up the tape for my hands.

Rex shakes his head. "Don't be a dick."

"I don't mind," the new guy calls. "Jay, you go ahead."

I smile at Rex. "Problem solved." I hand Rex the tape, but he doesn't take it.

"Stay in the ring, Lenny," Rex fires without looking away from me.

Lenny is halfway through the ropes but does as Rex says.

"Just let me hit the bag at least." Rex has rules—rules that I never break. Only one person in his gym at a time during training. He doesn't want any distractions. That's what makes him the best trainer.

Rex shakes his head again. "Hold out your hands."

I do, and Rex takes the tape from me. "You can work with Lenny."

I tut. "No. That's bollocks."

Rex raises a brow. "That or leave."

I glance at Lenny, who's looking very fucking happy with himself. "Fine."

Rex tapes my hands and slips on my boxing gloves. He hands me a helmet, but I climb into the ring without it. I don't think much is going to happen with Lenny.

Rex jumps up along the side.

"Lenny, I want to see you defend yourself. Don't strike back. All you do is protect your body." Lenny starts bouncing at Rex's words and nods. He smashes his hands together.

I look at Rex. A bag would be more beneficial than fighting Lenny, who won't be able to stand up too much. I bounce, too, warming myself up. Everything fades away. This is why boxing is a lifeline for me; it allows me to peel every emotion back. And today, after seeing Layla, I need this release more than ever.

I dance closer to Lenny. His hands protect his head. I keep my movements slow to test him, and then I strike at his ribs. I don't put much force behind the punch. He bends, lowers his hand, and protects himself.

"That a boy, Lenny," Rex cheers him on. "Keep focused."

"No cheering for me?" I ask as I fire a jab at Lenny's head. He protects himself again and dances away.

"Your ego is too big, Jay," Rex teases. I grin and fire off a few quick but light-handed jabs at Lenny, who blocks each one like a pro.

"You're good," I tell him.

He stops moving and smiles. "Jesus, Jay, thanks so..."

As he dribbles on, I hit him solid in the stomach. The force drives him back, and he hits the ground hard.

"Get up!" Rex screams, and I dance back as Lenny rolls to his knees, trying to catch his breath.

"Get up now, Lenny, or your training ends here for good."

Rex's words get Lenny up off his knees. His face is red and raw as he fights for air while holding his stomach.

"Never lose focus. It can be a compliment, it can be an insult, but don't let your guard down."

I dance around Lenny and take a few gentle swipes, which he blocks. I keep my hits low as he finally gets his breathing under control.

His hands aren't as high; my hit seemed to have knocked his confidence.

"Keep your fucking hands up," I bark at him.

He does.

"One little hit and you turn into a fucking woman," I smirk at him. "Pitiful."

"Jay," Rex warns.

I reach out and tip the side of Lenny's head. "Weak," I tease.

I don't anticipate Lenny's attack. One thing Rex warns us about is that no matter what, don't bring anger into his motherfucking ring. His words. So I don't expect it when Lenny barrels into me with all his strength. His fist cracks into my side, and I'm falling, but not before he hits me with an uppercut. My lip splits open, and blood pours from my mouth as I hit the ground. I recover quickly and bounce back to my feet.

"Didn't know Lenny the pussy had it in him," I tease as I wipe the blood from my chin.

"That's enough. Both of you get out of the ring."

I'm not done. Not even fucking close.

I step up to Lenny, ready to retaliate.

"Jay." The warning in Rex's voice has me backing away from Lenny. I look at Rex for the first time since entering the ring.

Yeah, he's pissed.

I shouldn't have come here.

Words rise up, but I swallow them and get out of the ring.

"You lost your control." Rex speaks to Lenny. "Never lose control. That's my number one rule, Lenny."

"I messed up," Lenny counteracts.

I remove my gloves and start peeling off the tape.

"Hit the showers," Rex orders Lenny.

"Good fight," I call after Lenny.

He glances over his shoulder at me and smirks. "Thanks, Jay."

Rex faces me. "You want to tell me who pissed in your cornflakes?"

Rex knows where I came from, but Layla isn't someone I ever discussed with him. He pulls off the rest of the tape for me.

"Are we still good for tomorrow night?" I ask. That's my official training day.

"Yeah, Jay. You can't just arrive like this again."

I pick up my sweater and pull it on over my head. "I won't."

Rex doesn't move as I wipe more blood onto my sleeve.

"If you ever need me, just ring. Like a normal fucking person." Rex grins as he holds out a fist. I bump it with mine.

"See you tomorrow." I leave the gym feeling more tightly wound. Once I'm in the car, I check my face in the rearview mirror. My lip still bleeds. My tongue flicks out and licks the blood. The cut stings, and I keep jabbing at it the whole drive home. The pain keeps me focused. It keeps my thoughts away from Layla for a short time.

Large white gates start to open. The ivy covers them, not allowing anyone to see into the property. My father values his privacy, especially after the scandal with my mother that still tortures him. I sink my teeth into my cut lip. Blood soaks my tongue, and I swallow the metallic liquid as I drive up to the house. Lights along the driveway have started to come on. It's only four, but it's already starting to get dark. By five, darkness will blanket most of the grounds. I pull into the six-car garage and turn off my car. I dab at my lip as I make my way into the empty house.

My father is never here, but a staff of servants moves around the house without making a noise. They seem to appear when we need them. The hallway is warm; two of the fires along the long wall have been lit. From the heat, I'd say it's been a while. A mirror that hangs on the wall soars twelve-feet high, stopping at the ceiling. The black outline is decorated in twisted metal petals. I take a step closer and examine my split lip. My father won't be happy with me showing up at the charity looking like I've been in a fight. He doesn't approve of my boxing but turns a blind eye to it. For now, that is.

"Good afternoon, Master Jay."

I step away from the mirror.

"Your father asked me to give you this."

I turn and take the small envelope from William's gloved hand. I open it in front of him, and he glances away, giving me my privacy.

Don't be late. We expect your arrival at 8:15. I would appreciate Alexandra being with you.

I push the note back into the envelope. A phone call would have gotten his message here quicker. Why my father insists on leaving me fucking notes is beyond me.

I nod at William, and he gives a bow of his head before I leave to go upstairs and get ready for the charity. I dial Alex's number, and she answers on the second ring.

"I'll be ready at seven thirty," she answers.

"How did you receive your message? By a carrier pigeon?" I ask as I climb the stairs before rounding the landing and making my way to the next set of stairs.

"A letter." I can hear the smile in Alex's words. "Hand delivered today by one of your father's servants." She pauses. "Don't be late." Her words no longer hold a smile as she hangs up.

I make it to my room to find my suit hanging up. The fire has been lit too, and my curtains drawn.

Anger laces through me, and I swallow it down, but it's like a yawn that's already formed. It leaves a lump in my chest.

I take out my phone again and pull up my private PI's number.

He, too, answers quickly.

"Jay, it's been a long time."

"I found her," I say into the phone. I'm picturing his bushy gray eyebrows rising into his fading hairline.

"A full refund will be given," he grinds out. He's a man who doesn't like to lose.

"She arrived at my college. Keep the money and get me her address. She must live nearby."

Some part of me hopes he says no, asks me why I want her address, and tells me that's a line he won't cross.

"Give me twenty-four hours."

My heart trips at the idea of finding out where Layla is living, and with whom.

"I want it by eleven tonight," I say.

There's a pause. "That's six hours."

I grin. "You better get to work, then." I hang up as my mind starts to conjure ideas of what I'll do when I have her address.

I need to leave her alone.

But I already know I can't. The moment she stepped into that gym was the moment I knew everything I had built up here was fucking useless against her.

CHAPTER FOUR

LAYLA

I T'S BEEN THREE DAYS since my first day of college, three days of numbness. I built up all my hopes of having a fresh start, only to have them smashed. To make matters worse, Evelyn received news about one of the kids from the foster home I grew up in.

My chest tightens as I think of Nelson, and I wonder yet again, for what feels like the millionth time, how he died. No one will give us any information about him. I want to attend his funeral, but without a second name and his location, that isn't possible. My mouth dries up at the thought that if the news had been about Jared, I don't know how I would have handled it.

I also came to the conclusion that Jay isn't Jared. Jared would never hurt me. My shoulders are marred by small purple bruises, but nothing feels worse than the fear he pushed deep inside me. So deep that it opened up old wounds.

The clang of Evelyn's knife on the white porcelain plate draws me back to the breakfast bar. I glance at Carl's empty chair. He's staying in Galway over the weekend. I push my cereal around my bowl. Evelyn's soft touch on my arm has my gaze jumping to hers. "He'll be back soon."

My face blazes. *Am I that transparent?* I get anxious when one of them isn't around, and an irrational fear shows up, telling me this perfect life that I've found myself in won't last forever. Evelyn tells me this self-doubt is normal, and these thoughts will fade. But they haven't.

"I know. I was just thinking about college," I lie, then I shovel a spoonful of cereal into my mouth. I chew, not tasting the food.

Evelyn's smile tugs at her mouth. "Layla, it's okay to worry about Carl. Honestly, he loves when we fuss over him." She rolls her eyes dramatically. "It would break his heart if he thought we weren't pining over him." Her words and batting eyelids have me smiling back at her.

"There's that smile," she says while gently stroking my cheek before tapping me on the nose. "You better get ready for school you don't want to be late."

I quickly check my phone. Yep, I am going to be late if I don't leave soon.

***

I park my car under low-hanging trees and have to run into the college as the rain pelts the asphalt with a violence that sends the water spraying back up. The fabric of my black trousers soaks up the water. I clear the three steps and make my way into the building, dripping wet.

The hallway is empty—I'm late. The receptionist glances at me. Her gaze trails to the small puddle of water that's started to form under my feet. Her nose curls before she turns away.

I hurry and make my way to my business class. I give a quick whispered apology for being late and sit down. I take out my notepad and pen, which survived the onslaught outside, and take notes for the next hour and a half. My clothes have dried out somewhat, but they still feel damp against my skin.

I spot Ashley a few times during the day, but each time, I duck my head. Today, I don't want to talk to anyone, and missing three days of class has pushed me even further back.

After the news of Nelson, school didn't seem to matter—until it did. Until I could see the concern and worry in Evelyn's eyes, and I couldn't disappoint her any further.

My body collides with someone, and I stumble back, but I catch my balance at the last second.

Alex glares at me. "You did that on purpose." She brushes off her designer sweater while tilting her head. Her face holds a smile, but her words aren't friendly.

"Sorry, I wasn't watching where I was going," I stutter.

She shakes her head, and two girls who appear as perfect as she does flank her on either side. "Clearly. They're really starting to let anyone into Kingscourt." She speaks to the girls as if I'm not standing in front of her.

Move, Layla. I sidestep Alex and her friends, but she blocks me.

"Watch where you're going next time, scar."

My head snaps up, and her smirk grows while her gaze travels to my legs like she can see all my scars, even though they're covered.

I brush past her and hear their laughter the whole way out of the building. I don't stop until I'm in my car.

The drive home is haunting. Memories of Bert's anger and violence resurface with a vengeance. I push his face away while fighting the tears. Seven years of therapy, then one insult from a pretty girl sends me into a tailspin. The news of Nelson is the real reason, but it always takes that one small thing to tip a person over the edge: the tip of the iceberg, the icing on the cake, the last straw, the straw that broke the camel's back. That is one of Evelyn's favorites. The heaviness lifts slightly as I think about Evelyn saying it; she was so serious, and the saying made me laugh hard even as my body and soul cried from all the pain.

I'm home quicker than I expected. By the time I walk into the house, exhaustion pulls heavily on my shoulders. I take a deep, calming breath before going to the kitchen. Evelyn takes off her reading glasses and glances at me. She has so many questions burning in her eyes. Why am I home early? Was I crying? How was college? Her khakis and loose cotton blouse make her look like she belongs on a beach, not in a kitchen reading some thriller.

She settles on "So how was school." as I get myself a glass of water.

My throat has utterly dried up. I gulp the water until the glass is empty, and only then do I turn to Evelyn. "Interesting." That's the best I can do, but as Evelyn continues to watch me, I have the urge to tug at my ear to give my hands something to do. "I'm just tired. Honestly, it was a lot. You know, missing so many days. But I'll catch up. I'm really enjoying it."

Evelyn tilts her head before her mouth rises, forming a pleasant smile. "Good. That's really good, Layla."

Lowering my gaze, I fidget with my bag, which is still slung over my left shoulder. Placing it on the counter, I glance at Evelyn and nod. "I'm going to take a shower before dinner."

"Okay, sweetheart."

I take the opportunity to leave without any further questioning.

"Layla." I stop at the door, glancing back at Evelyn. "I'm so proud of you."

I inhale deeply, and a weird feeling pulses through me. I find myself standing a little straighter as Evelyn beams at me. "Thank you." The words are low, but from her smile and nod, I know she heard me.

The spray of the water helps my aching shoulders. Lathering my hair, I try not to think about the day I just had, but I can't stop the memory playing out in my mind. Ruminating is something Evelyn warns me about. Yet I can't stop the memory of Jared that assaults me.

It's the cold—the cold that seeps into my back and runs so much deeper than my twelve-year-old brain could truly comprehend.

A coldness that, after seven years, has never left me. I fear it never will. My lids squeeze closed as the memory tears another piece of me apart.

Scorching heat burns my face, and it's no match for the cold slate floor that penetrates through the back of the light, flimsy white dress.

Bert's hand rises again but stops in midair, every finger straight to the point of straining. My eyes shoot from his hand to his red face, flushed with anger and alcohol. I'm waiting for the blow. I'm waiting for a reaction so badly. I want it to happen and for this to be over.

The front door behind Bert is stark white. Why I focus on the door, I'm not sure. It becomes a beacon that seems to grow smaller the longer I lie there waiting. My gaze darts back to him, and his hand connects with my face. The burn seems worse than the first time. My head whips to the side. Darkness clouds in quickly, and I welcome the blackness, only for the veil to disappear and keep me rooted in the here and now. The spindles on the stairs take priority in my mind. My eyes trace where some of the white paint has been chipped off from all the children that have passed through the doors of Bert and Ronnie's foster home. Each breath I take hurts as I force the air into my lungs—lungs that never seem satisfied.

"I asked you a question!" Bert's voice isn't slurred or fueled by the anger clearly displayed on his sixty-year-old face. His words are a command. A prelude. A promise that isn't idle.

When he asked me where his car keys are, a fear developed deep down inside me because I don't know. And if I don't answer soon, he will continue to beat me.

My hands tremble as I try to push myself up from the stone floor. Bert's eyes are wide, and he tilts his head. A threat for me to hurry up screams from his tight features.

"I don't know," I say honestly. All the while, my body curls in as it braces itself for the next slap that Bert plants on my face without hesitation. This one is harder than the last and sends

my head snapping back. Blood fills my mouth, and stars fill my head. It takes me a few seconds before my hearing slowly starts to trickle back. On reflex, my hands touch my aching face.

Bert steps closer and leans over me, stumbling slightly. If he falls, his sheer size will smother me. But he catches himself and continues to bend down.

"You think you're clever?" he snarls.

My shoulders hunch forward as I try to move away. It's a movement, a tiny movement, one he won't notice.

He notices. Oh, no, no, no...

He reaches for me, and my shoulders draw closer together as I dip my chin into my chest. His large hands easily encase my small wrist, and he applies pressure that threatens to shatter my bones. A scream that I can no longer keep in is torn from my lips at the same time the front door opens.

He's taller and broader than I am. I can't see his features with his black hood up, but I'd know him anywhere. I know that his eyes will be tight around the edges.

My body sags with relief. Everything will be okay now. Jared is two years older than me, but right now, he's like a giant filling the doorway. Bert releases me and is focused on the door.

"Get away from her." Jared speaks each word through heavy breaths. Bert spins toward him, and Jared's body stiffens. A new fear enters my system; the dread drips slowly down my spine. What if Jared got hurt this time? The thought pulls a whimper from my lips.

"It's okay, Layla." Jared's reassurance is spoken as he stares at Bert. All I can do is nod at him.

"It's okay, Layla," Bert mimics, and he sneers as he lingers for what feels like forever but is only a moment. Then he gives me one final look before leaving Jared and me alone in the breezy hallway. Jared's steps are measured as he walks slowly to me while pushing back his hood. His brown eyes are soft

as he kneels down and reaches out carefully to take my hand. His fingers entwine with mine, and all my bones sigh at the contact.

"It's okay, Layla. I'm home."

My lips wobble at his words, and before I can respond, he pulls me into a hug that, at first, is too tight. My groan has Jared loosening his hold on me, but he doesn't let me go, and I let all my guards down and inhale. Everything feels right, and all I smell is Jared.

Even with the blare of the TV and the constant threat of Bert's anger, right now, I am safe. I am home. I am with Jared.

My heart thumps heavily in my chest as if I've just relived that moment all over again. I'm a mixed bag of emotions and try to think of Evelyn's words about ruminating. I need to think about the positives.

"Three positive things," I say while taking water into my mouth, nearly causing me to choke. I move my head out of the spray and let the warmth hit my back so I can speak without drowning.

"I survived my first few days of college. Ashley seemed nice." I hesitate, searching for a third positive. "I didn't look hideous in my gym uniform." I let my head go back under the spray so I can condition my hair.

I feel better when I leave the bathroom and enter into my adjoining bedroom. The carpet under my feet always makes me sigh with contentment. The full-sized bed takes up most of the room, and my desk sits neatly under the window that overlooks the front garden. The best thing about the room is the walk-in closet. I flick the light on and pull out a clean pair of pj's.

Once dressed, I face the mirror to brush out my hair. Even wet, the color still looks light, and the strands reach my waist. Dropping the brush on the dresser, I leave my room and go downstairs.

Evelyn is still reading her thriller. When I arrive in the kitchen, she takes off her glasses and puts her book down. "I'll get your dinner now, sweetheart."

"I'll grab it. Go read your book."

Evelyn picks back up her glasses. "Thanks." She sinks her attention back into her reading. She's such a bookworm; she devours up to three books a week. I place my dinner in the microwave and grab a soda before sitting down at the table. As soon as I'm seated, my phone dings. It's Morgan.

How was your first day at your swanky college?

My fingers quickly glide across the letters. **Great. It's a regular college.**

I turn the phone over as I eat my dinner; the click of the soda can is the loudest sound in the quiet house. My phone dings again, and I ignore it so I can focus on my food.

"Who's that texting you?" Evelyn glances at me over the rim of her glasses. Her glee at me texting someone has me picking up the phone.

"Oh, it's Morgan." I force a smile while looking at Morgan's message.

How boring. Want to go out tonight?

"She's such a lovely girl," Evelyn says.

"Yeah, we're going out tonight."

Evelyn tries to tone back the dial on her sunshine, which beams at me. But it's still way too strong. "Great. No curfew. You go out and enjoy yourself." Evelyn picks her book back up. Her excitement is evidence in her lack of parenting. But I'm not like most girls my age. I never drink, and I always come home early.

I reluctantly answer Morgan's text. **Yeah, where to?**

Just be ready at nine.

I place the phone back on the table while pushing my food around the plate. My appetite just took a run and jump off a cliff.

✱✱✱

Morgan doesn't arrive until nine thirty. I grab my bag and race from the house while Evelyn stands at the door, waving me off. I can see the girls in the back of the car snigger as I approach. I've met Morgan's friends once or twice, but I always forget their names.

"In the front seat, L." Morgan rolls her window down and waves at Evelyn.

I give one final glance to Evelyn before climbing into the car. I feel like a kid being coaxed into a kidnapper's vehicle—the sweets I'm offered aren't worth the aftermath, yet I go anyway.

For the millionth time in my life, I do something I don't want to.

CHAPTER FIVE

LAYLA

"LET'S GO." I SNAP my seat belt into place, and Morgan beeps the horn as she drives away. I'm so underdressed, but I always am. Morgan looks presentable from the window. Her red dress has a high neck with long sleeves, but it's cut off, barely covering her behind. Her long tanned legs go on forever. My skinny black jeans and green blouse look so bland and ugly compared to these girls. Both of her friends are dressed to kill in halter dresses.

"So, where are we going?" I ask as Morgan pumps up the music. The thump of the beat penetrates the dashboard. Crossing my arms, I try not to fidget or look behind me as the girls in the back whisper and giggle. The smell of cigarette smoke lingers, the scent making my queasy stomach more unsettled.

"Woodview Estate in Mullagh. A guy I know is friends with a guy who lives there." Morgan looks at me for the first time. The flick of her gaze across my outfit is done with raised eyebrows.

Shifting in my seat, I turn more toward Morgan. At that angle, I can slightly see one of the girls in the back. Our eyes clash, and she winks at me. The car feels too warm suddenly, and I open the top button of my blouse.

"I have a curfew, Morgan," I lie. Woodview Estate has a bad repetition. It's one thing going there during daylight hours but another thing to go there at night. Her vagueness on who is hosting the party causes a tightness in my chest.

More sniggers erupt from the back. Morgan glances at her friends in the mirror with narrowed eyes. "I'll have you back in time. Relax, Lola," Morgan replies.

Wow!

"My name is Layla," I say through gritted teeth. I sit back and face the window this time.

Morgan mutters, "Sorry." The streetlights soon thin out as we leave our small town and make the short journey to Mullagh.

"Oh my God. Les just texted." The music is switched off, and Morgan bounces in her seat, glancing from the mirror to the road.

"What did she say, Bonita?"

"Mindy is drunk and she kissed Deco."

Morgan inhales a sharp breath while both girls squeal in the back with excitement. I don't know who Mindy or Deco are. All I want is for this night to be over so I can go home and climb into bed and tick off this outing. I won't have to do this again for three more months. That's the silver lining.

"What a tramp!" Bonita says, tilting my seat slightly as she pulls herself forward. "I mean, she was only with Kieran, like, last week."

Morgan inhales deeply again at the scandal. "Oh, I thought he was seeing you, Bea?" Silence fills the car as the tension grows. I hide my grin as I look out the window.

Finally, Bea laughs. "No, I dumped him ages ago. Me and Kieran are history from, like, really far back. So far..."

Well, that isn't transparent or anything. Morgan and Bonita overlook Bea's hurt and lies. They start slashing Mandy—or is it Mindy?—instead. The poor girl really takes a bashing.

The house we pull up to doesn't look like one that's hosting a party. From the road, no lights shine from any of the front windows. Morgan turns down the music as she pulls in along the curb.

"Is this it?" Bea speaks up from the back. I glance at Morgan, curious too. Maybe I'll get lucky and the party will be called off. She's scrolling through her phone.

"Does it say number six?"

I wait for one of her friends to check.

"Layla!" Morgan pokes my leg.

"Sorry, I didn't think you were talking to me." I look at the number hanging beside the door. Yep, the gold number says six. I relay this, and we all climb out of the car. Shifting from foot to foot, I clutch my bag.

As Bea and Bonita climb out of the back of the car, I get my first proper look at them. They look like hookers.

"Morgan, are you sure?" I have a bad feeling about this place. The girls giggle behind me while linking arms with each other.

Morgan reaches for the buttons on my blouse and unbuttons two more before trying to wrestle my bag from me.

"You look like a granny. Give me the bag," she snarls at me.

I pull my bag back, having enough of her. "Better than looking like a hooker." I say the words before I can think. Bea drags in a sharp breath. Morgan stands back, and shame burns my face.

"You're just jealous," Morgan seethes.

"I'm sorry, Morgan. I shouldn't have said that."

"I'm freezing. Can we go inside already?" Bea jumps up and down in her tiny outfit, her boobs almost pouring out of her dress. I don't want to go into the party, but standing outside on a dark night in the middle of an estate isn't the brightest idea.

Morgan gives my bag one final look before clicking her fingers. "Let's do this, bitches."

I fall into place behind them. A shiver crawls up my back and prickles my neck. *There's nothing wrong. You're overreacting like always.*

The closer we get to the house, the clearer the music and voices become—my pulse spikes.

Morgan knocks on the door.

"Is my lip gloss still on?" Bea asks Bonita, who pouts her own lips before answering.

"Yeah, you look hot." They bump hips.

Morgan knocks on the door again before pulling down her dress. The action is pointless since every step she takes allows us all to get a view of her white thong.

"You're hot too, Bonita," Bea says.

I'm focused on the door and praying that no one answers Morgan's insistent knocks.

"Maybe we should go," I say just as the door opens.

The scent of something stronger than cigarette smoke seeps through the air. A guy much older than we are leers at Morgan and her friends. His eyes skim over me with disinterest. After cracking his tattooed knuckles, he opens the door wider. His three-quarter-length shirtsleeves showcase his tattooed arms. Some tribal ink rises from the collar of his red-and-white checkered shirt and disappears into his brown hair, which is cropped close to his head. A scar that runs along the left side of his skull is stark against his dark skin.

"Come in, ladies," As each girl passes, he checks out their rears with a smirk. As I pass by him, I quickly glance at him before looking away. I curl my shoulders in, hoping it will discourage his wandering eyes.

The hall floor is concrete except for a few threadbare rugs strewn around the place; no smiling family fills the empty, crooked picture frames that hang over the radiator. A light flickers overhead as we enter the kitchen, where most of the partygoers are. Sweat makes a path down my back. The small room is crammed. I huddle behind the others, and for the hundredth time, I wish I had stayed home. This isn't the usual type of party Morgan brings me to.

"Morgan!" a guy shouts excitedly while jumping off his chair. He nearly topples a girl to the ground who'd been perched on his lap. The girl gets her balance and thankfully doesn't fall. She stands out from the rest because of the pink stripes in her hair. The guy embraces Morgan, his hand groping her behind at the same time. Bea and Bonita get called over by two guys who lounge at a small yellow table. Two ashtrays filled to the brim hold burning cigarettes. Too many cans and glasses litter the table. Both guys wear black wool hats, which gives their eyes a hooded and dangerous look. As I quickly glance around the room, all the boys look the same: tattoos, baggy jeans. They all watch us now.

"Kieran, take your hands off my ass," Morgan says to the guy hugging her. His blond hair and sun-kissed skin look so out of place from all the other males. I feel like I've stepped into the wrong house. Out of the corner of my eye, I see the guy who let us in take something out of his pocket and slip the small bag into another guy's hand. I press my arms along my side, trying to make myself appear small as the guy from the door latches his eyes onto mine. I try to swallow, but my throat is too dry. He looks away, moving on to the next guy and passing him another small bag of powder.

"Hi, I'm Kieran."

I blink at the hand that's held out to me. I take it and follow the tanned fingers to their owner's light blue eyes.

"You want a drink?" he asks. I shake my head, taking my hand back before glancing around at everyone else; they've all fallen into place with someone. The music is a low hum that makes all conversations unintelligible.

"Everyone here is really nice," Kieran says to me. He holds up his hands, and a grin spreads across his face. "Don't judge until you get to know me." Kieran's lips twitch into a full smile. I want to tell him to leave me alone, but he's the safest bet. It isn't his appearance that makes me think he's the safe bet; it's how he makes me feel. I don't feel unsafe.

Everyone else looks like they're from the wrong side of town, and I'm pretty sure they're all high, whereas Kieran seems to be just slightly drunk. The girl with the pink stripes in her hair keeps watching us. I think it's Mindy, the one the girls spoke about in the car.

Kieran talks and doesn't seem to mind having a one-sided conversation. I nod but keep my eyes on the girls. A few times, the guy who let us in catches my eye; his stare is unsettling. I swallow, but my dry throat can't take much more.

"Could you get me a glass of water?" I ask Kieran.

His eyes light up with surprise. "You talk?"

I force a wobbly smile. "Yeah."

He nods enthusiastically before getting me a glass of water. I force myself to loosen my death grip on my handbag by slinging it over my shoulder. I try to appear more relaxed.

Kieran returns, smiling while holding my glass of water. I examine the contents before taking a deep drink. The glass is empty when I return for air.

"Do you want another one?" Kieran's brows knit together.

"Yeah, please. My throat is parched," I explain lamely. When he returns this time, I drink slowly, my eyes skimming over the brown kitchen and worktops that seem to only hold alcohol and mixers. There is no toaster or kettle—no signs that this house is used every day.

"You have beautiful eyes," Kieran compliments me.

He catches me off guard, and I choke, spewing some of my water on him. "Oh God. I'm so, so sorry." I start dabbing his shirt with my hand.

"It's fine." Kieran smiles. "You don't take compliments well?"

My cheeks heat with embarrassment, making me stop what I'm doing. "What?" I ask.

"I complimented your eyes, and you spat on me."

I drop my hands and try to calm my beating heart. I'm coming across like a nutjob. "Thank you, Kieran."

"You're welcome... You never told me your name."

"Layla."

"What a beautiful name for a beautiful girl." He takes my hand and presses a soft kiss to it.

"Where is the bathroom?" I ask.

Kieran tells me the bathroom is upstairs—the first door straight ahead. He even kindly offers to accompany me, but I decline. Before I leave the kitchen, I look for Morgan. She is very... occupied.

The hallway is empty. As I go down the hall to get to the staircase, I notice a door to my right that I didn't pay attention to when we first came in. I hear voices in the room, and one in particular tickles at my memory. I pass quickly and walk quietly but briskly up the stairs. The bathroom is old and simple but surprisingly clean. I do my business before washing my hands. I look up into the mirror and meet four sets of wide blue eyes. The crack runs in a zigzag down the whole mirror. What caused the crack? A smash of a fist? Maybe something else?

The cut-off screech of a female has me freezing. I listen, but there's only silence. I take a tiny step toward the door, pause, and listen again. I can hear someone whisper. I stare at the door, unable to move.

Pull it together, Layla.

I open the door to a scene that has my body going still, but my mind goes straight into reverse, to a twelve-year-old Layla, who has no scars on her leg. Time can heal so much, but not that. Never that.

"What are you staring at?" The question snaps me back to the present, and my shoulders tighten. The guy who opened the door holds Bea by the throat. The red marks promise to bruise soon. Her mascara runs down her face as she looks at me with a plea for help.

Tattooed fingers snap in my face, and I stumble back.

"Are you stupid?" he barks. I hate that word. I've been asked that my whole life. I shake my head; my words have disappeared again. He lets Bea go, and she runs down the stairs without looking back at me. Now I have this guy's full attention. A tremble builds violently in my hands.

"You don't look right to me," he says as he takes a step closer, his eyes traveling up and down my body. His lips curl into a snarl. "What are you doing here anyway?" His stare is full of suspicion.

I shrug. *Say something, Layla. Please.* I look at the ground, hoping he'll leave me alone. His hand curls around my face, and I whimper. Forcing my head up, he tightens his grip on my face.

"You open your mouth to anyone about me, and I will cut out your tongue."

I nod as fear from all angles builds up inside me.

"Chester." This voice is one I remember.

Chester releases me and glances down the stairs at Jay, who stares up at us with a wrath in his eyes that makes me shiver, and I have no idea if it's directed at Chester or me.

CHAPTER SIX

JARED

FUCK ME. SHE LOOKS like a virgin in that getup. I want to defile her.

"What's up, man?" Chester raises his head as he speaks. He's still too close to Layla for my liking. He shouldn't be breathing the same air as her.

I grip the banister. "The boys want you."

Layla hasn't moved. Her chest is still, and I question if she's breathing. What is she doing here?

"In a minute." Chester looks away from me.

My hand tightens on the banister, and it creaks under my grip. "Now, Chester."

His focus is back on me. He grinds his jaw, but he nods as he walks away from Layla, giving me more relief than I should feel.

Chester juts out his chin and narrows his eyes in question as he makes his way down the stairs. I stop him before he passes me. "Don't ever put your hands on her again." My voice is low, deadly.

"If you so say, Jay." Chester doesn't like my request.

I grin. "I do say so."

He fights a snarl, and I let him pass me before I allow myself to do what I really want, which is beat him to within an inch of his life.

Layla doesn't move as I release the banister and take a step up toward her. "What are you doing here?" I growl.

Her chest rises and falls rapidly. Her pink tongue flicks out and wets her lips. Her mouth is small but perfect. I can imagine it around my cock.

"I'm here with friends." Her voice is stronger than I expected.

I continue to climb the stairs. "What friends?" I sneer.

She folds her arms across her chest. "My friends."

I grin as I clear the last step and tower over her. "I thought I told you to stay out of my way." I dip my head while pushing my hands behind my back. They demand I hurt her, but I deny that want for another that is so much deeper. The one that has liquefied in my veins, manifesting as something so primal—the urge to protect her.

I fucking hate it.

I want to defy the need to protect her.

"I'm going." Layla ducks her head and tries to get past me. I don't move, blocking her access to the stairs. Now I'm wondering which waster she's with downstairs.

Anger accelerates my thoughts, and they scatter as I step closer to her, stealing the last of her personal space. She won't look up. She's staring at my chest. The pulse flickers rapidly in her neck.

"You can go when I say you can go."

Her head lifts up to me. Her blue eyes drink me in and pierce something inside me that twists my gut.

I hate her.

My hand leaves the confines of my back, and I'm touching her hair. The strands are as silky as I remember, and I lose myself in my primal instincts and lean in, inhaling her scent. She takes in a sharp breath at my action, but I don't give a fuck that she's watching me sniff her. Everything in me stirs to life, and her lips become my sole focus.

I want to fuck her.

I want her.

My mind becomes consumed with someone else fucking her. Someone else fucking what they have no right to touch. My hand tightens on her hair, and she hisses in pain.

"Who are you here with?"

"I told you. My friends."

I tug a little harder and draw her closer to me. Her legs brush mine; her breasts press against my chest. My body is aware of every single inch of Layla, and my cock becomes a rod of steel. "I want names."

"Morgan and her friends," she stutters.

I loosen my hold but don't release her hair. I like her this close to me. "This isn't a good place to be."

"I've realized that." Her sharp words brush my cheek.

I release her, but I can't step away from Layla. She fucks so badly with my head that I can't even think straight.

"Layla." A female voice behind me should have me stepping away, but I can't.

"I don't ever want to see you here again." I keep my voice low as I issue the warning and step away. I don't go back down the stairs but brush past her. I ball my hands into fists so I don't reach for her again.

She rushes down the stairs. "Are we going?" Layla's voice is panicked.

"Yeah, Bea wants to leave."

More female voices fill the hallway before the front door closes.

"Where did Layla go?" I hear a male voice a few minutes later, and I have to control the speed at which I arrive down into the hallway.

My lips stretch across my teeth. "Who's looking for Layla?" I ask.

A blond guy is holding a plastic cup of alcohol and points it at himself while wearing a fucking grin. "Me. And you are?"

"Kieran, go into the kitchen." Chester pushes Kieran's chest, and he stumbles back, spilling his drink across his shirt.

I need to leave before I allow the violence to pour from me. I turn and pull the front door open. I don't bother to close it behind me.

"Yo, Jay!" Chester calls after me, but he can fuck right off. I've parked my car down a side lane at the end of the housing estate. Chester has warned everyone not to touch my vehicle. They listen to him. Here, he is the king—just not to me. No one rules over me.

I get in, and I find myself driving in the opposite direction of my home. After a while, the group of houses I'm starting to become accustomed to seeing comes into sight. The small white fences all in a row tell me I'm close to hers.

I slow down as I near Layla's home. I have no idea if she's there, but I allow myself to picture her safely inside. The front bedroom is hers, and I watch the dark window for a while. I sit until a light comes on in her room. My heart thumps loudly in my chest as she appears; it's a split second as she pulls the curtains. She doesn't look terrified in her natural habitat. She's Layla. She's beautiful. I find myself smiling, and then her face is gone, the curtains blocking out the light, and I look away as the smile leaves my face. Then I drive home.

***

When I arrive back home, Alex's car is in the driveway. *What the fuck does she want?* I park in the garage and enter the house. Like always, William appears in the hallway.

"Ms. Alexandra is here to see you, Master Jay."

I'm waiting for William to tell me where she is.

He clears his throat, looking uncomfortable.

"Where is she?" I have to ask.

"In your quarters, Master Jay."

I don't linger but make my way to the third floor, which my father gave me to live in. I only use about one-third of the floor that spans across the entire mansion.

I find Alex flicking through a magazine in the sitting area. She's wrapped in a dressing gown.

"I don't recall scheduling a sleepover," I say, holding back my irritation.

She continues to flick through the magazine pages. "We never finished what we started at the charity event." Alex drops the magazine and stands up. She pulls the band out of her fake blonde hair, and all I can do is compare it to Layla's naturally straight blonde locks. Everything about Layla is natural. I grit my teeth as Alex opens the dressing gown and lets the material pool on the ground around her stilettos. The red lacy set doesn't leave much to the imagination. The red stockings cover her legs, and she takes a confident step toward me.

"Like what you see?" She reaches me and pushes up on the tips of her toes to press a kiss to my mouth. I turn my face away, and she doesn't like that one bit.

Touching my belt, I wriggle it open. She grins and falls to her knees. I push my jeans and boxers down and take my cock in my hand, stroking it a few times. I picture blue eyes flashing with fear, and my cock starts to grow. I remember the feel of her hair, the smell of her skin, the brush of her breasts against my chest. My cock is painfully hard. A warm mouth wraps around my shaft, and I groan as I picture Layla on her knees. I grip Alex's head and push her further down on my cock until she gags. I hold her there for a moment before letting her back up.

"You like that, Jay?" Alex's voice pierces any illusion I've created.

I glance down at her as she looks up at me before taking my cock in her mouth again. I nudge her away, my cock dying, and I give it a few strokes and look away. I conjure up the image of Layla again. I'm picturing her sprawled out on my bed in a black lacy set. I grip Alex's head and push her back down on my cock. I approach Layla, and she smiles up at me. All I want to do is bury myself in her. Alex groans and pulls me out of my fantasy. I force her head quicker over my cock so it won't die. I've never had a problem holding an erection, but ever since Layla showed up, the only thing that makes my cock stand is her.

I go back to my fantasy of Layla and fast forward, burying my cock inside her. Layla moans, and a groan slips from my lips. I pump faster and harder, wanting to empty myself in her sweet pussy. I pound fiercely and Alex gags, but I stay with Layla as I grip Alex by the hair to keep her lips locked over my cock as I fuck her mouth hard. I groan again as Layla's face twists with ecstasy, and my seed pours out of me. I give a few final jerks and release Alex's head.

She crawls away from me, coughing and gasping. "What the fuck was that, Jay?" She's wiping my seed off her face with the back of her hand.

"A great blow job, Alex." I wink at her and pull up my boxers and jeans.

She gathers herself off the floor. Alex looks at me, ready to complain again, but no one invited her here. I buckle my belt and don't look away from her.

She stands straighter and picks up her dressing gown, wrapping it around her body before heading to the bathroom. I sit on the couch that Alex just vacated, and it's easy to pull up the image of Layla again. My cock twitches but quickly dies a few minutes later as Alex enters the room. She's dressed and is stuffing her gown and shoes into an overnight bag.

"Not staying?" I tease.

"I'll see you at school tomorrow." She flicks her hair across her shoulder and holds her head high.

I salute her with two fingers, and she leaves me in peace—before it turns into something dark. I get up and leave the room. The farther I walk across the third floor, the heavier the weight grows on my shoulders. A part of me wants to stop this, but I grin as I pull the chain from around my neck and unlock the door with a key that hangs from it.

I step in and close the door behind me. The room bursts into light as I flick the switch. Her face is everywhere, in every available space in the room that once was a servant's bedroom. I step up to my most recent one. It captures Layla perfectly. I had the curve of her nose wrong before, but now she's perfect. Pictures I've drawn of her over the years coat the walls. A lot are from memory, but soon I started to wonder what she would look like as a woman. I didn't get much wrong, just the nose. I touch the most recent picture; it's her standing in the gym, the look in her eyes. So haunted, so tormented, and that's what I drew. That look that I know all too well.

When my father found this room, he looked at me with the most disturbed expression on his face.

"This ends now, Jay. If it doesn't, you are getting help." He speaks while looking at the pictures of Layla. "I have tried to find her, but she's gone. You need to let her go."

The pencil snaps between my fingers. She isn't just a girl. No one will ever understand. I don't think even Layla understood what she was to me. I can't face my father. This addiction is like a cancer that's eating away at me, but no matter how painful it becomes, I don't want it to stop.

I've lived my whole life in chaos, and my father wants calm. I don't know what calm feels like.

"Jay. You bury this here, right now. Jared and Layla don't exist."

My vision blurs. He has no idea what he's asking of me.

"You. Are. My. Son." His hand touches my shoulder, and I shrivel under the contact. "Why do you cower from me?" My father's question carries hurt and confusion. Those emotions are like friends of his when they come to me. He has tried to penetrate the walls that even I can't seem to bring down.

I spin and face him. Anger roils through me, twisting me, and I want to lash out.

He sees it. "Control yourself. You are a McGivney. You do not lose control." He pushes my chest. "You do not cower."

I blink tears that spill as I fight for control.

My father's voice lowers. "We do not seek anything or any-one." He looks around the room, his voice lowering further. "We do not obsess. We are powerful just as we are." He reaches me, and this time, I don't cower as he grips my neck. Pain leaches out of him.

"You are my son," he reminds me.

I'm a shadow of a person—a shadow of his son. I fight a fresh wave of tears as I try to show my father that I am the man he needs me to be.

He releases me and nods, taking one final look around the room. "This ends." My father's gaze is still unsettled, and the longer he glances around the room, the more naked I feel.

"Yes, Father." My admission has him nodding and leaving the room.

I didn't lie that day. I locked up this room and all my pain with it. That is, until she showed back up. Three years of not obsessing. Three years of not feeling. Three years of touching this door but never entering this room. Three years of keeping my promise to my father.

Three years smashed in a second.

CHAPTER SEVEN

JARED

"Have you heard the rumors?"

I don't respond.

"Jay?" Alex's tone holds annoyance.

I look at our group as I sit on the hood of my car. My mind is still stuck on Layla. I spent most of last night obsessively drawing images of her from different times I've seen her on campus. I've scoured my memory from watching her home, and I drew her standing at the window of her bedroom, her hands raised as she grips either side of her bedroom curtains, ready to pull them together. Every time I've seen her, I've drawn the moment, capturing her face perfectly.

"What rumors?" I ask, not giving two fucks as I slide off the hood of my new BMW. I try to keep my Layla watching to a minimum, but I scope out the parking lot and campus grounds for her every few minutes.

"You okay, man?" Mark stuffs his hands into his letterman's jacket pockets. Navy and white stripes run down the arms. The crest of Kingscourt College is printed in bold gold on the front.

"Yeah. So, what rumors?" I ask again and try to appear present. Alex is watching me with narrowed eyes. I grin at her, my gaze skipping to her mouth, which I fucked last night. She's not one bit amused, and that entertains me.

"Coach was caught with one of his students." Mark dishes the dirt with a smirk.

"Who?" Warren asks while lighting up a cigarette. He's the only person in our group who smokes, and he doesn't wear the college jacket like the rest of us. I think Warren likes to think of himself as a rebel of some sort. He's from money, but as far as I know, it's pretty fucking dirty money. He's an O'Reagan, and around these parts, that makes him untouchable, so I'm happy to have him in our group.

"Not sure. I think her name was Lucy or something." Mark shrugs and digs his hands deeper into his jacket pockets.

"Maybe he'll bring her to the dance next month." Alex smiles sweetly. There's nothing sweet about her. I try not to stiffen as she links her arm with mine. "No one will steal our crowns."

Abby and Caroline smile at Alex. She could vomit on the ground, and they'd be in fucking awe of her. How have I not noticed how annoying this group is? For the last three years, I've moved through my day on autopilot. Was I happy? Maybe. Numbness gave me some reprieve from the constant throb that had returned since Layla's arrival, and with it came a huge fucking appetite for pain.

I untangle myself from Alex and rub my hands together. It's cold, and I've had enough of standing around—my eyes snag on a blonde running across the lawn. A guy lingers close to her. Too close.

I'm already walking away.

"Where are you going?" Alex barks after me.

I spin and walk backward. "Some of us have class," I lie.

She knows my schedule. I'm sure William even gave her a blood sample on my father's instructions. Alex doesn't call me out, though. Public appearances and all that bullshit, and I use that to my advantage as I walk toward Layla, who's nearly out of my reach. I have no idea what I'm going to say, but I have this urge to be near her. This constant need to be around her never seems to lessen. Even when I'm close to her, it doesn't go away. I'm not sure what would make the ache stop. My cock twitches. Having her fully might.

She disappears inside the building. The guy who was trailing behind her reaches the main door, but I grip him by the collar of his sweater and spin him around so he's facing me. The front door slams closed as his hand slips off the handle.

"Why are you following Layla like a fucking stalker?"

He tries to pull out of my hold. "Get your hands off me."

I smirk and lean in. "Make me."

He tries to pull away, and I let him for a few seconds, until I get bored and shake him, cutting off his protests.

"Fuck's sake. She's friends with my sister, Ashley. She asked me to keep an eye on Layla."

I don't like his answer. I shake him again. "Why?"

He tugs, and I release him. He shrugs his shoulders. "Ashley didn't tell me why."

I'm watching him, searching for lies.

"You need to relax, man."

Relax? I take a threatening step toward him.

"Mr. McGivney."

I turn to the dean, who raises a brow and two fingers, beckoning me forward. I give the boy a death glare, and he leaves.

"Dean."

He inclines his head. He holds no love for me, nor do I for him, but my father has placed both of us in his pocket, so I do the dance and follow the dean to his office.

"The anticipation is killing me," I say flatly as he opens his office door. What bullshit assignment does he have for me now? Give a speech to the school on the importance of grades? I've made too many of them in my three years at Kingscourt College. I'm sure I could squeeze a few more out, especially since I would be addressing Layla too. If I were addressing the whole college, that is.

The dean's lips tug up, his eyes filled with smugness. I follow his gaze and take in my father. It's my turn to give a smug smile when the dean reacts to seeing my father sitting in his chair.

"Frank called me about your attendance."

My smile would have grown at the look on the dean's face, at my father using his first name, but my attendance isn't something I thought would be brought to my father's attention.

I face the dean. "You could have spoken to me," I say through my annoyance.

"He spoke to me," my father interrupts. "It's one thing paying the teachers for your grades, but with your attendance, we can't make every student not remember you were missing. Having one hundred percent attendance is imperative. So, three days in a row isn't something we can make disappear." He stands.

"It's only three days." I hadn't missed a day in three years. So what the fuck did it matter?

"Where were you?" My father walks around the dean's desk and toward me.

"You could have asked me this at home."

"I was in the area when Frank called."

The dean wisely says nothing.

"You weren't with Alex, because she was here. I've checked."

My heart starts to race. My father is watching me closely. I spent three days staking out Layla's house because she was missing from her classes. My father has no idea that she's even here, and I can't let him find out.

"I wasn't well," I finally say.

My father reaches me and lowers his voice. "You weren't at home. We checked all the footage."

I shrug and try to stay calm. "So what? I took three days off and blew off some steam. I'm sorry," I add at the end.

My father holds my gaze. "Why don't I believe you?"

The dean clears his throat. "We can mark off several students from his class for a three-day field trip."

My father nods without looking away from me. "Whatever you have to do, Frank."

"Don't do that," I say. "They didn't miss class."

"You should have thought about that before you decided to fuck up your perfect attendance." My father's jaw tightens.

I have to look away to control myself.

"I'm going to be late for my meeting. Frank, I will leave it in your capable hands to clean this mess up."

"Of course, Mr. McGivney."

My father doesn't say goodbye as he leaves the dean's office. I'm ready to follow him out the door when the dean stops me.

"What was your business with Lucas Garcia?"

I clench my jaw before I speak. "Who?"

"The boy outside just now. Lucas Garcia. The one you were speaking to."

The one who was stalking Layla. I'm not in such a rush to leave now that I have a name.

"His sister, Ashley, asked me to keep an eye on him. Some kids were bullying him."

The dean sinks down into his chair. "That's very admirable of you, Jay, to look out for people less fortunate than you." His words are sincere. "He and his siblings are here on scholarships—which your father pays for. But I'm sure you already knew that." The dean's words aren't so sincere now.

Fuck him.

"Yeah, keeping an eye on my father's investments."

The dean leans forward in his chair and starts rearranging his desk. "Best to leave him alone."

Is it now?

"Of course, Frank."

He bristles at me using his name. "You can leave now, Mr. McGivney." His words are sharp.

I leave his office. The hallways are thronged, and everyone is moving outside. I can hear the rapid beat of propellers.

I'm making my way outside, but I already know what I'm going to see.

My father is rising high above the school in his personal helicopter.

"Wow, someone has a helicopter here?" a boy says beside me.

"Maybe the president was visiting?" a girl says beside him.

I'm pushing through the crowd. On the other side of the helicopter pad is Layla, shielding her eyes as she looks at my father. If he looked down, would he recognize her from all the drawings in my room?

I'm not sure if Layla can sense my gaze on her, but she looks away from the helicopter that still captures everyone's attention and over to me. Her chest puffs out with a sharp inhale before she shifts back into the crowd and out of my sight.

CHAPTER EIGHT

LAYLA

I'VE BEEN AVOIDING EVELYN since coming home from the party with Morgan last night. But I don't think I can avoid her again today. I wish I could, as I'm extra frazzled after seeing Jared again. He brought up too many emotions in me. Each time I see him, I don't really see this guy—Jay. I see my Jared; I think he's in there somewhere. I'm just not sure how to reach him. Each time Jay corners me, one emotion seems to rise above all the rest, and it surprises me. I want to be brave. Brave for Jared.

After placing my key in the door, I open it slowly. The TV sounds softly from the living room, so I become a coward and close the door gently before tiptoeing up the stairs and into my room. I tie up my hair and enter my bathroom. Running the taps, I splash my face with water as my bedroom door opens. A surprised Evelyn comes in as I dry my face. "How was last night? You broke curfew," she says with a broad smile. Like me coming home later than eleven is great. I have no idea what time I got home, but it felt late.

Guilt has me gripping the towel—*small white lies.*

"It was fun," I say. I keep my back to her while slowly folding the towel and placing it back on the rack. It gives me a chance to gather myself before facing her.

When I turn around, Evelyn watches me carefully. "You know you can talk to me about anything."

I've shared my darkest secrets with Evelyn, and she and Carl have helped me, saved me. But I won't let them down. I *will* be a typical nineteen-year-old. I force a smile. "It was fun. Really."

Evelyn starts picking up the clothes that I dumped on the floor last night. "If there was a boy there, you could talk to me about that." She glances up, a smile playing on her lips. Once again, I don't want to let her down.

Taking a deep breath, I smile. "Well, there was this one guy."

My clothes hit the floor as Evelyn claps her hands. "I knew you were hiding something. Tell me."

Am I really going to do this?

"His name is Kieran." I tell her all about him, only I place him in a fancy house with friends who look just like him—the surfer kind and not ones who look like they would rob you. Everyone laughs and dances, and it's all fun and games.

Evelyn takes my face in her hands. "I am so happy for you. *You* deserve this, Layla."

My eyes burn, and my throat contracts. Turning away, I move to my bed.

"Thanks. I better get started with homework," I say as I climb onto the duvet and drag my book bag closer to me. I open the flap of my bag and start taking notepads out. When I glance at Evelyn, she's smiling. I fidget with the notepad, wanting nothing more than for Evelyn to go. She does, giving me a kiss on the forehead before finally departing. She pulls the door closed, and I'm alone. My mind wanders to the dark place, where it tells me I'm not worthy of Evelyn and Carl. I'm lying to them.

Small white lies, I remind myself. I get off the bed and walk to my window. I often think I see a car across the road watching me, a car very similar to the one I've seen Jay drive. Right now, no one is there. Another thing I'm sure I'm imagining.

I return to my bed and throw myself into my work. This is how I spend the rest of the night.

***

Only a handful of cars dot the parking lot; it's still pretty early. Facing Evelyn this morning wasn't something I was up to after lying to her. My focus had been consumed with my schoolwork, but once I stopped, guilt churned painfully in my belly most of the night, making sleep come and go in broken spells.

I get out of the car and am surprised when I meet Ashley halfway down the hallway. I avoided her yesterday, but today that doesn't seem possible. She grabs my arm and steers me down a small corridor.

What have I done?

Ashley lets me go and swivels around to face me. "Look, I'm going to be really straight with you." She takes the same stance she had with Lucas and Sam only days ago—one hand on her hip, her head swaying to each word.

I force myself not to take a step back. My bag's strap slips slightly off my shoulder, and I push it back up.

"What you do with your free time is your business," she continues, "but I know you were at Chester's over the weekend." She pauses while lowering her head slightly, as if egging me on to answer but not giving me a moment to gather my thoughts. "Those guys are into some really heavy shit, and I don't want to see you getting hurt. You getting what I'm saying?" With furrowed brows, she stares at me.

"I'm going to make a lot of assumptions. Like Chester is the house owner?" I pause, and Ashley nods. "I'm also going to assume the heavy stuff is drugs?" Another nod. "And you think I would take drugs? Just to make it perfectly clear, I would never." As I speak, my voice lowers. I'm trying to defend myself without letting anyone else hear.

"You look like a really nice girl, Layla. I'm surprised you were even there. But looks can be deceiving." Her tongue runs along her teeth.

"I was surprised too. But you have nothing to worry about." I want to get to class. I don't need thoughts of Chester swirling in my mind. There's a tense moment of silence between us, which consists of her staring at me and me clutching my bag strap and trying to stand still without fidgeting. Finally, we both relax, and the tension breaks.

"I'm on cafeteria duty today, so I'd better get started." That ends our awkward conversation. I'm ready to bolt, but she's been so good to me.

"Want some help?" I ask.

She smiles. "I'd appreciate that. It's just preparing for the morning rush."

Ashley doesn't mention Chester again, and we spend the next hour getting the cafeteria ready. I never thought cleaning could be so relaxing. But the silence of the school and the soft overhead music relaxes me. We finish early, and Ashley comes over to me as I'm putting away a brush. Ashley is really nice; she smiles a lot as she speaks. I'm a bit surprised to hear she has a baby, considering she isn't much older than I am. Her love for her son, Nicco, shines through her words. He's twenty months old. She never mentions the father, and I don't ask.

As we gather our bags, I feel relaxed enough with her to ask the next question. "How did you know I was at Chester's?" Saying his name feels wrong, like saying Candyman in the mirror. I find myself glancing over my shoulder so that I can look back at Ashley. Her whole demeanor has changed at the mention of his name, and I regret asking.

"Sam was there. One of the other guys was asking about you."

It must have been Kieran, but why was he talking about me? I find myself smiling. Maybe it wasn't an untruth I told Evelyn after all.

Classes go by quickly, and no matter how many times I tell myself I'm not looking out for Jared, I know it's a lie down to my core. I finally spot him outside with a group of people who seem captivated by what he's saying. His profile has me entranced. His wavy black hair is cut short, showing his tanned neck. The black T-shirt stretches across his muscular back. My heart thumps as I think of a boy from years ago. His jeans are faded on purpose and not from being washed too much. He's over six feet tall. The boy he reminds me of causes a pain in my chest.

I continue to watch as he rocks from heel to toe. I used to make fun of him for that, and he never got mad at me no matter how much I teased.

The bang of the main door drags my attention back to here and now. Ashley slings her bag across her back and looks up at me.

"Are you okay?" she asks for the tenth time today.

"Yes. I'm just tired," I answer. The daylight is starting to fade, and the evening is slowly crawling in, throwing a dusting of darkness across everything. The shadows look like bottomless pits, and I shiver while shoving my hands deeper into the pockets of my red jacket. It was one long day at college.

Everything in me stills as Jay walks toward me, his face tightening the closer he gets. It transforms him from someone I used to know with dimples and light eyes to an angry god.

"Hi." I sound breathless as he stops in front of me.

He glares at me and rubs his jaw before speaking. "The three days you were missing... Where were you?"

He's angry.

My throat aches again; my heart beats rapidly as I stare up into the dark abyss that wants to consume me. I need to speak, but for the first time with Jared, the words are lodged in my throat.

His large hand touches my jawline, and my eyes flick up at him. His stare has darkened even further, and I'm not sure what prompted him to touch me. He looks revolted by the action, yet he hasn't let me go. When we were younger, I knew exactly what he was thinking, but right now, that unknown is scaring me.

His hand travels down to my neck, his thumb flicking back and forth. His touch burns into me. I swallow.

"Where were you?" He looks at me with haunted eyes.

CHAPTER NINE

LAYLA

"Jared." My voice sounds like a plea, and he drops his hand from my face, but the depth in his eyes doesn't disappear. It feels like I've just woken up as I look up and notice Alex. Her lips are pursed.

"So, I'll see you tomorrow?" Ashley's words are drawn out, making me acknowledge her. A brow rises with a question, and I don't blame her. I pivot toward her so I don't have to keep staring at Jared. She glances between him and me.

Heat burns my cheeks. "Yeah. I'll see you tomorrow."

"Three whole days is a long time," Jared says, and my attention reverts to him. He still stares at me with a thousand memories. He rubs his jaw as the tension grows.

Alex folds her arms across her chest. Her nostrils flare, and all I want to do is walk away, but I can't seem to make my feet move.

"Are you going to introduce us?" Alex's words are clipped.

But once again, Jared stares at me. "This is Layla," he blurts. My lips twitch.

"Yeah, I remember her from gym class. But how do you know each other?" Alex's gaze trails down to my trousers, reminding me of my scarred leg.

My chest caves in. I need to leave. I dip my head, not able to keep Jared's stare much longer. "I better go." Pulling the strap of my bag up, I glance at Jared and regret it almost immediately.

His jaw is tight, his eyes narrow. I can't stand how he's looking at me, so I walk away.

"I asked you a question." His angry outburst seems to surprise Alex as much as me. Her eyes widen, and I find myself hurrying away.

Racing to my car, my hand searches my bag for my keys, and when they land on the cold metal, I yank them out.

"You're running away from me?" He's right there, his voice controlled, like I had imagined his earlier eruption. I stop to take a calming breath before turning to him. His hands are jammed in his jeans pocket, and I can see the thirteen-year-old Jared. There's a small vulnerability underneath his hard surface.

"No, I'm not running. But I don't owe you an explanation. You said..." I look behind him at everyone who watches us. "You said to keep out of your way."

He steps closer. "Now I'm asking you. Where were you those three days?"

"What does it matter to you, Jay?" My voice lowers to a painful whisper. "You aren't him."

He takes a step away from me. His jaw clenches, a muscle working away. He doesn't leave.

"You're you, but you're not."

"Jay?" Alex calls, and he glances at her over his shoulder before looking back at me.

I'm standing in front of someone who said we were forever. That no matter what, we were stuck with each other. But now I'm a stranger to him, and I don't know why he wears such a look of hate.

"Jared," I say softly as memories have me wanting him to be Jared.

His sneer rattles not just my hand, but it bounces and throbs right down to the core of what made up Jared and me. My hands shake as I try to get my key in the door.

He's still behind me, and my hands continue to rattle, but I manage to unlock the car. I climb in and grip the steering wheel, and his large frame bends so he can look in at me.

"This isn't over." His words are said like a promise. He reaches in and pries the keys out of my fingers. I'm waiting for him to drag me out of the car and demand that I answer him. Instead, he slides the key into the ignition.

He closes the door, and I put all my focus toward the windshield as I watch his departing form from the corner of my eye. My stomach twists as I turn the key. I reverse, and my eyes lock with his. All I see is Jared. Pain latches on to my soul, and like a vulture, it tears strips off me. Pulling away from him is the second hardest thing I've ever done in my life. The first was losing him to begin with.

You can cry now, I tell myself, but no tears come. Instead, laughter bubbles up my throat and passes my lips.

"Jared," I say. "Jared." I speak lower this time. My throat burns; my eyes sting.

The ringing of my phone cuts through the silence. I rummage in my handbag with one hand while focusing on the road.

"Hello," I answer.

"I was worried about you." Evelyn's voice is a wake-up call.

"I got caught up on campus," I tell her while hitting my indicator for the next left-hand turn. "Sorry, I should have called," I add.

"That's okay, sweetheart. You're on your way now?"

"Yeah. I'll be home in ten minutes."

Evelyn says her goodbyes, and I throw the phone down on the passenger seat.

Pulling into the driveway makes me question everything that has happened since I started college—believing I had found Jared, agreeing he was Jay, and now knowing it's him. I don't linger in the car; I'm already late.

After opening the front door with my key, I call out a hello and get two in response from the kitchen. My chest tightens. Should I tell them? Something in me says not to. I remove my red coat and hang it on the white freestanding coat rack that was only delivered last week. It finishes off the hallway nicely—oak floors and beige walls, while the small hall table and now the coat rack are white French furniture. The walls are decorated with so many photos of us. From the zoo to just random days at the house, Evelyn seems to capture every moment. I feel like a traitor.

Evelyn stands at the island, making a sandwich. "Take a seat. I'm making you one too." She points the knife at my usual spot in the kitchen. I take a seat, letting my bag slip off my shoulder and onto the arm of the chair.

Carl joins me, giving me a cup of tea. Sugar and milk already sit on the table. Why do I feel like a stranger all of a sudden?

"How was your day?" Carl asks while stirring his tea. His freshly shaven face has a gleam to it. I thought the beard suited him better, and so did Evelyn, but neither of us ever said it to him. He thinks he looks younger, which he does, but a beard just suits him more.

I sugar and milk my tea, giving myself a moment.

"Good. I had lots of classes. I had to stay late to catch up on some notes," I say as Evelyn slides the plate across to me before sitting herself down with a steaming mug in her hand.

I take a bite, and while I chew, I decide what to disclose. They don't seem to like Jared, and right now, my emotions are all over the place. I need to assess them and be more stable before I speak of him. I can't bear them being negative toward him, and I also don't want to disappoint either of them.

"I made a friend." Volunteering information is always a good tactic if I don't want them to ask questions.

Evelyn raises an eyebrow. "Well, is he or she in one of your classes?"

"Yeah, and she's really nice." I find myself smiling, thinking about Ashley.

"Do you have class tomorrow?" Carl asks. "I want us to have a family day."

"Could we move it to Monday?" Evelyn requests. "I have a lot going on tomorrow."

My phone buzzes in my bag, and my heart jumps. I tell it to calm down. After taking a few bites of my sandwich, I look up to find Evelyn staring at me, a smile on her face.

"Aren't you going to check that?" she asks, clearly delighted that someone is contacting me. When I don't, she continues. "It might be Kieran."

Heat scorches my cheeks, and I actually groan while glancing at Carl. Yep, he's going to have the talk.

Getting the phone out of my bag, my chest hitches. I have a message from an unknown number.

I want answers.

I'm staring far too long at the three words.

"Kieran?" The hope in Evelyn's voice has me looking up. I glance again at Carl.

Tiny lines form around his eyes as he smiles. "It's okay, Layla. You're a young woman now." He pats my hand, and I want to crawl under the table for so many reasons. They both wait for my answer. I look down at the message again. I close my phone.

"Yeah, it's Kieran." I've never seen Evelyn so excited. She covers her mouth with her hand as she continues to smile.

Carl gives my hand one final pat before getting up. "Just... Evelyn will have a chat with you." And there it is—the chat about the birds and the bees. I don't look at Carl. He sounds as embarrassed as I feel.

"Going to catch up on some football," he says.

"Okay, love." Evelyn removes her hand as she watches him leave. Her nod to him tells me he's mouthing something. I turn just as the door clicks.

Picking up the second half of my sandwich gives my hands something to do. I have no appetite now. The feeling of betrayal causes a thickness in my throat.

"It's okay, Layla."

My head shoots up at Evelyn's words. Does she know I'm lying? Am I that obvious? I can feel the blood drain from my face. "What?" I ask, finding it hard to keep her gaze.

Her eyebrows furrow. "I'm not going to have 'the talk.'"

The fact that I wasn't caught has me releasing the sandwich back onto the plate, and I force a smile. "Oh. Thank God."

Evelyn observes me carefully. "You look really pale."

"I'm always pale, Evelyn," I say with the lamest laugh ever. My hands hug the mug.

Evelyn nods, the tension leaving her shoulders. When she smiles, the crinkles around her eyes appear. "When do we get to meet Kieran?" I must have paled more, because Evelyn laughs. "I'm joking," she says while standing and taking her mug to the sink before coming back to me.

"We'll see how it goes?" I say, and she nods before looking down at my half-eaten sandwich.

"Are you finished?"

"Yeah, thanks." I pass her the mug before taking my phone off the table. "I'm going to take a hot shower, get some studying in, and maybe have an early night."

"Okay, sweetheart." Evelyn speaks from the sink. A part of me wants to walk across the kitchen and hug her, but I don't want to alarm her. I slip out of the kitchen, and when I have my foot on the bottom step of the stairs, my bag slung over my shoulder, and my hands gripping my phone, I realize I should say good night to Carl since I didn't intend on coming back down.

I push open the door to the den, and Carl looks up at me. His dark eyes hold mine for a brief moment before he quickly returns to the TV.

"Just wanted to say good night. I have lots of studying to do, and then I'm going to get an early night in," I say.

He looks relieved, as if I might be here to ask questions that would make both of us uncomfortable. "Well, good night."

He opens his arms, and I walk over to where he sits, bending at the waist to hug him. Closing my eyes, I relax, and a lump forms in my throat.

"Night, Carl," I say before leaving the hug. I don't want to start bawling all over him, but it's not until now that I realize how much I needed a hug from someone I know who loves me.

Finally, in the safety of my room, I sit on my bed and open the message again.

I want answers.

My fingers trace the message. It's Jared. Funny how I found him. Tears burn my eyes, but they don't fall. I want to say so much, but words sometimes aren't my friend. They get lodged in my throat, and afterward, I would kick myself for not saying something.

I miss you I type and then delete it.

Thank you for always saving me. I delete it.

I'm only here because of you. I delete that as well.

I don't send anything, but I save his number. Something tells me to save it as Kieran, but Evelyn and Carl never look at my phone. Secondly, lying to them isn't right. I'll leave it for a few more days, then tell them it all went south with Kieran and tell them about Jared. My stiff shoulders relax, and I start to feel less guilty about lying to them.

"Come here." I hang my head, letting my hair cover my face as I make my way to Bert. His friend's eyes follow me as I cross the room. "Get up here." He pats his knee like I knew he would, and I don't hesitate to sit on it.

My legs touch the ground. I focus on Ronnie's black boots. They remind me of something from the movie Hocus Pocus. The toes curl up at the ends. She would fit in perfectly with a bunch of witches. Her large frame and constant laugh make people see her as harmless and jolly, but behind the smile is a witch. One who doesn't like children, just the money she gets for them.

"Sing a song for Richard." Bert's breath brushes my hair, and the alcohol fumes are enough to make me look away. I flick a glance up at Richard, who leers at me. My skin crawls.

"Sing 'As She Moves Through the Fair.'" I don't want to, but I know better than to say no to Bert. In front of his friend, he won't hit me, but he will humiliate me. Then afterward, he'll hurt me. Closing my eyes, I picture my favorite person in the world. I wish he was here right now. If he were, he would stop this. With one eye open, I take a quick look at all the horrible faces, and none of them are Jared.

"Don't drag it out," Ronnie says, her eyes narrowing. She hates any attention that Bert gives us. Her jealousy is unfounded, but she justifies it somehow in her twisted mind.

"Shut your mouth," Bert shouts at Ronnie. I curl in as much as I can, my heart picking up pace.

"Sing!" he barks, and I close my eyes and picture Jared while I sing. The room is silent until I sing the final note. I open my eyes, and everyone claps.

"Fucking brilliant, isn't she?" Bert slurs his words. His praise makes me never want to sing again. He takes the good out of everything. But it is my own fault. I should have never allowed him to hear me sing. I thought the house was empty as I cleaned, but he was there listening, and now this is my punishment every time his drunken friends come over.

"Off to bed with you." Ronnie speaks then and takes a deep gulp from her beer can. "You've school in the morning." I don't move until Bert bobs his knee—that's his permission to leave. I do, with my hair hanging in my face.

"You're good people taking in a simple minded kid." Richard speaks before I'm out of the room. My face burns. "But she can sing," he adds.

I take the stairs two at a time. The green carpet is worn down; the small red flowers that once were vibrant are now faded. I enter my room quietly. Two single beds face me, both covered with the same patchwork cover. Riley is usually asleep in bed long before I am. Her long brown hair splays across her pillow. She's two years younger and doesn't really speak. She goes under the radar in the house, and it annoys me. I'm jealous of how invisible she can become. Maybe one day I will be too.

I take off my clothes and hang them on the large wicker chair at the end of the bed before taking my nightdress out from under my pillow. After getting dressed, I slip into bed, the cold sheet a welcomed sensation on my still-burning skin. Pulling Jared's sweater out from under my pillow, I close my eyes and say my prayers, thanking God for Riley, Nelson, and Jared. I pray that I will find a better home, maybe somewhere with trees. I love trees.

With that thought, I fall asleep and dream of wild forests and running through long grass, while the smell of Jared makes me feel safe.

CHAPTER TEN

LAYLA

MORNING COMES QUICKLY. I spend too much time sitting in the parking lot rereading the message.

I want answers.

I want answers too, but I don't think I'll get them—all the answers to too many questions. I can assume the answers will be painful, anyway.

Why did you not try to find me? Maybe he had finally gotten rid of me, and he was glad that he didn't have to save Layla again. I'd been a noose around his neck that he was free of.

I squeeze my eyes shut before opening them, like I can erase that last thought, which terrifies me. Jared is better off without me. I seem to bring pain to the people I love most.

I shake my hands out as I get out of my car and make my way to the main entrance of the college building. Once I make it all the way to the back hallway, my shoulders slump as a bitter smile moves my lips. *He wants answers.*

I tell myself I'm overreacting and need to calm down. Maybe the message isn't from him.

"Morning."

I jump at Ashley's voice.

Ashley holds up her hands at my reaction. "Wow. Jumpy, are we?" she questions while dropping her hands.

Yep. I need to relax. Five minutes in, and already I'm acting like a nutjob. "Sorry. I didn't sleep well," I say honestly. The large dark circles under my eyes are my evidence. I follow

Ashley out into the main corridor. My gaze darts around the space, searching for the large frame of Jared, but no one is here yet.

"So... yesterday?" Ashley makes her way to our first class. She moves her notebooks from one arm to the other. She doesn't glance at me as she speaks, and I'm grateful as a flush creeps across my cheeks.

"Yeah, that was awkward," I blurt out.

Ashley turns back to me, her eyebrows raised. "That's an understatement."

My toes curl in my shoes as the tops of my ears burn.

"How do you know Jay?" Ashley narrows her eyes slightly, her lips puckered as she hugs the notebooks to her chest while waiting for my answer.

I shake my head. "I don't." A puff of laughter escapes my lips.

"You really don't know him?"

"Yes, and no. I knew Jay from a few years back, but we were kids then." It's hard using the name Jay. We were kids who lived with abusive people, who damaged young children to a degree that functioning in our adult life is still a challenge.

"It looked pretty intense." Ashley doesn't shy away.

A heaviness settles on my chest. She has no idea.

"What about his parents?" I ask.

Ashley's hands tighten on the notepad, her stance more rigid now. "Honestly, everyone knows Jay's father, Mr. Mc-Givney. He practically pays for the school. My family and I are so grateful to him. I wouldn't be here without his scholarship program."

My stomach sinks. What are the odds for me to arrive at a school that Jared's father owns?

"His mother?" I ask.

"I'm not sure. Rumor has it that she's dead, but that's not definite."

A fluttering starts in my belly as Alex stands in front of us. She's alone.

Her gaze is fixed on me. Her hair flows down her back in thick blonde waves. The cut-offs she wears showcase a pair of long, tanned legs. She wears deep red lipstick that defines her mouth.

"Alex," the warning in Ashley's voice has me wanting to run.

"I'm only here to say hi and introduce myself properly." She glances at me now. Her gaze is hard, even as she smiles. "I'm Alex. Jay's girlfriend."

My lungs constrict, making breathing difficult. She's beautiful, and they're perfect for each other. A stunning couple.

"Hi," I manage to say back without sounding as devastated as I feel. There's an expectation heavy on my chest, like I should say more. But that's the best I can come up with.

"He told me he knew you when you were younger."

A wash of dizziness makes me reach out for the wall I'm standing beside. I nod my head as I stare at my hand touching the wall like the paint is the most interesting color of magnolia I've ever seen. He spoke about me—confirmation that he's Jared. He's really Jared. That knowledge hits me harder each time. The weakness in my muscles steals me of any remaining strength.

"I get it. You're like his little sister." Alex continues to twist the knife. "I'm cool with that."

I nod again. "We don't really know each other anymore." My voice sounds squeaky as I remove my hand from the wall.

Alex tilts her head with a sly smile on her lips. "Are you calling Jay a liar?" Those red lips continue to rise, and she appears gleeful that I would call Jared a liar.

"Alex. She's not calling anyone a liar. All she's saying is she hasn't spoken to him in years, so leave her alone." Ashley moves in front of me. "We have a class to get to," she says to Alex before turning to me. "You've missed enough already." She raises both eyebrows while nudging her head to the left, telling me to go now, and I do so without glancing back.

Slumping against the wall once I'm out of sight, I let my rattled heart settle.

Here is Jared, with a girlfriend, a family, and friends. I don't wish I had never met him because I honestly don't think I would have survived, but I hate messing anything up for him. I push off the wall. Ruminating isn't allowed—number one rule of Evelyn's.

Classes go by slowly, and I find myself not being present during the lectures. No matter how many times I read the text in front of me, I can't fully comprehend the words. The moment the class ends, I make my way outside. The air is crisp, and I don't want to go back into the building for afternoon classes. I throw my bag in the passenger seat of the car.

"Are you hiding from me?" At the sound of the male voice, my heart threatens to come right out of my chest. The first thing I notice is Lucas's slightly damp hair, as if he just showered. The second is the brown paper bag in his hand. A large silver watch catches the light, getting my attention for a moment before my eyes travel to his soft brown eyes.

"No. Why would I be hiding from you?"

He holds up the brown bag. "Okay, correction. Are you hiding from Ashley? She's worried."

I exhale. "I just needed fresh air."

I want to ask what's in the bag, but Lucas smiles.

"You are avoiding my sister, and I get it." He walks a few feet away and sits down at a bench. "She can be a lot at times."

"I like Ashley."

Lucas grins and unrolls the bag. "Sit down. Join me."

I don't have anywhere else to go, and I don't want to be rude. I slide in across from Lucas and stuff my car key into my pocket.

"Peanut butter sandwiches," he says, holding one out. "Take one."

I'm staring at the sandwich.

Lucas laughs. "I didn't make them—Ashley did. So you won't get food poisoning."

"I'm okay." The smell of peanut butter is strong, and a thousand memories assault me.

"Please? It will make Ashley happy if she knows you ate one of her sandwiches."

I swallow the lump and reach out and draw up a sandwich. I've avoided peanut butter. It isn't exactly something that was an intentional decision, but more on a subconscious level.

I take a bite, and it's everything I remember. Each bite is painfully joyful. So many memories of Jared smiling at me as I waited at the table for him to bring me my sandwich. He would cut off the crusts achingly slow, a grin on his face, knowing he was torturing me. Peanut butter sandwiches were food for our battered souls.

The bread grows heavy in my mouth, and my vision blurs as I look up at Lucas.

He looks horrified. "That bad?"

I try to swallow, but the bread is lodged in my throat. I don't have a minute to compose myself as a shadow looms over our table.

I can't process anything as Jay reaches out and grabs my arm, pulling me from the table. I'm ready to protest, but I'm so astonished as he continues to drag me further away from Lucas, who sits there with a look of pure shock on his face.

No words pass my mouth as Jay yanks me across the lawn. A few students glance our way and whisper, but no one intervenes.

"Get off me." My words have no impact. Jay doesn't slow down. A brand-new BMW that I know is his comes into view. He spins me just as we reach his car.

"Are you ready to give me my answers?"

I try to pull my arm out of his hold, but his fingers are too tight. Jay towers over me, and my words get swallowed up.

His eyes darken further, and his lip drags up. "You want to make this hard?" He looks past me at the school. "Fine." His grin stretches; it's like watching a shark circle blood.

We're moving around his car, and before I have a second, I'm in the passenger seat, and he's getting into the driver's seat.

"What are you doing?" My brain catches up with the situation as I reach for the door handle. The lock snaps into place, and my head turns back to Jay, who has started the car. "What are you doing?" I shout louder.

A booming bang grabs my attention. Alex has slammed her hands on the hood of the car, her gaze on fire with rage. I pull at the door handle again, but it's still locked.

"Let me out," I demand. Jay ignores me and revs the engine. I sit back as Alex removes her hands from the hood.

Her mouth moves. "What are you doing?" She asks the same question I did; only hers is said with a snarl. Her gaze leaps to me and pierces me with heat. If the sharpness were real, I would bleed out right now in the passenger seat.

Jay revs the car again, and Alex jumps to the side. He doesn't give her a second before he slams his foot down on the pedal, and we launch forward and out of the school gates.

CHAPTER ELEVEN

JARED (Eighteen hours before)

WHEN I ARRIVE HOME, it's not the silence that makes me pause in the grand hallway; it's William's absence. He normally materializes like a phantom with some update or request. Today, there's nothing, and that makes me edgy as I make my way to the top floor of the mansion. I'm still disturbed by my father's earlier arrival on campus. I'd been stupid and careless, but Layla's disappearance had burned so deeply that I needed to douse the flames and find out where she was. I dump my bag on the floor and make my way to my bedroom. After pulling my sweater over my head, I hit the double doors with both hands, and they swing open.

I stop advancing into the room and pull my cell out of my jeans. I got Layla's number when the dean was out of the office, and I grin as I stare down at her name in my phone—where it belongs. I write a text.

I want answers. I hit send and slip the phone back into my pocket. I'm ready to continue into my room. I'm not sure what makes me pause; the draft on my bare flesh, perhaps. I step away from my bedroom and pull my sweater back on. My father stands with his back to me. His hands are shoved into his black suit trousers pockets. He hasn't entered the room, but his head bobs from side to side as he takes in all the new artwork of Layla. "She's at your school."

William's vanishing act makes sense now. Fear strikes hard and fast and makes my steps falter.

"Layla Masters." My father glances at me and wears a look of fondness on his face, which fucking confuses me. "Silly of me, really. I should have known she would come for you eventually."

What happens now? That's the question I want to ask. Guilt weighs down my shoulders as I step up beside my father. "I kept my word for three years."

"Three years? Is that how long it's been?" My father's voice sounds foreign to me; it's the undercurrent, something I've never heard before.

"Father..." I start to explain, but the words die on my lips.

"She's beautiful. I can see the fascination." He looks at me with that odd fondness in his eyes. "Beautiful and dangerous."

"Layla isn't dangerous." I defend her straight away and regret it immediately as his spine straightens.

"I had my son for three years, and I knew recently, I had lost you again." He points at a picture of Layla on campus, hugging her books to her chest. Her hair is loose, and her eyes are wide and filled with fear. "To her."

He turns away and steps out of the room. I don't follow him. I'm fully aware he hasn't taken more than a few steps before he stops.

"She knew where you were all this time. She knew your name. She knew the college you attended. Layla might come across as innocent, but she's very dangerous."

Pain oozes into my being, and I turn to my father, wanting him to take back his lies. "Don't hurt her," I plead.

His gaze hardens. "She was missing the same three days you were. Was it because of that boy?" His anger heightens his words.

"What boy?" Is Layla seeing someone? The thought is fuel to my veins, and it only elevates my rage. I have no one or nothing to fire it at, so the rage boils in my blood.

My father turns his back on me. I want to scream and demand he tell me all about this boy.

"You look like a man possessed." His voice is low.

I relax my fists and stretch my aching fingers.

"She only wants your money, Jay."

"I don't have any. And Layla—"

My father swings around to me. "Don't be so naïve. All this…" He swings his arms wide. "It's all yours—no one else's. You are the sole heir to not millions but billions. You have to see what's at stake here. In four months, you turn twenty-two, and I plan to pass it all over to you."

He's making Layla out to be a gold digger, a vindictive one. Could she have known that I was here? What took her so long to find me? The thoughts of this other boy start to consume me again.

I blink and look up, but my father is gone. I have no idea how long I've been standing here fighting with the demons in my head.

"Father?" I call. Silence bounces back to me.

A throb along my neck has me looking back at the room filled with images of Layla. I walk inside, and with a lot of willpower, I close the door and turn the key. I want to look at her, but I also need the distance before I explode. Placing the chain around my neck, I know this room isn't sacred anymore. My father has a key and I never knew.

***

The next morning, Alex is waiting for me. I already know it's about Layla. I think I left everyone wondering what was going on with my outburst yesterday. Maybe that's what tipped my father off. My display was stupid and out of character. I'm sure Alex ran to my father.

I bury everything—all the hate I feel for Alex that tries to consume me—until there's an odd silence in my head. The habit from years of training myself not to think or feel returns like a blanket across my shoulders, and I get out of the car.

"Good morning," I greet Alex.

"I need to know what's going on with that girl. Layla?"

I lock my car and walk to Alex. With a nod, I speak. "Layla and I knew each other as kids. She moved away, and our friendship ended."

Alex folds her arms across her chest with a look of satisfaction. "When you were kids?" She smirks.

I continue to walk to Alex. "Exactly."

Alex's smirk turns into a full smile, and she links her arm with mine. "For a moment, I thought it was something more."

There's a question in her statement. I grin at her. "I was just surprised to see her."

"Where did she live?"

I thought my replies would have Alex losing interest, but clearly, she hasn't. I stop walking and face her fully. Digging my hands into my pockets, I lean in close to her face, only an inch between our mouths. My lips drag up. "Don't tell me Alexandra is feeling threatened?"

She scoffs as her gaze travels to my mouth. "Hardly. She hasn't got anything on me."

I step away. "Then you have nothing to worry about." I walk off, and Alex doesn't fall into step beside me. I move through the hallway taking fist bumps and pats on the back from guys while I return the smiles and shy *hellos* from girls. It's not until much later, when I see Layla sitting with Lucas Garcia, that my facade cracks wide open, and I lose all composure. I forget every trick I learned to conceal what I feel; I forget everything. All I see is Layla.

She's looking at Lucas with wide eyes as they share fucking sandwiches. My control shatters, and I reach the picnic bench and drag her from the table. I want to grab her face and make her soak up all my rage, but I pull her across the lawn. A few students glance our way. I fire a warning to each set of eyes I meet, and they stay fucking seated. I need to let her go. I need to gain some control.

"Let go of me." Her voice is strong. Too strong.

I spin her around so she's facing me. "Are you ready to give me my answers?"

She tries to tug away from me, and I tighten my hold on her. She knew where I was all along. She's looking up at me with fear etched into her stunning face.

I dig my fingers a little deeper into her arm. "You want to make this hard?" Someone walking toward us catches my eye, and I look past Layla, my gaze snagging on Alex. This should be my warning to calm down, but I can't. I want answers. I turn away from Alex and continue to my car. I try to be gentle with Layla as I place her in the seat. She's stunned, and her shock buys me time as I run around the car and get in.

"What are you doing?" Fear grows thicker in Layla's voice, and she reaches for the door. I push down the lock, stopping her from leaving, and she faces me. "What are you doing?" Her words are filled with dread, and I soak them up.

A bang grabs our attention as Alex slams her hands on the hood of my car. She's pissed. She knows this is more than what I told her.

Layla starts pulling the handle again, but she can't get out. "Let me out."

I ignore her and glare at Alex as I rev the car.

She narrows her eyes but removes her hands from the hood and stands straight. "What are you doing?" Her lips form a thin line. She swings around to Layla, and the way she looks at her has me revving the car again in warning.

Fury flashes across her features, but she still has her wits about her and steps to the side. I don't give her a second before I floor it, and the car roars out of the parking lot.

"This is madness." Layla's words grate along my heart.

I grip the steering wheel as I push the pedal to the floor. We lurch forward as the car tears down the road. "Slow down." She grips the overhead handle.

Without thought, my foot lifts slightly from the pedal, and the car slows down, but we still make it to the lake in record time.

Layla's silence the rest of the journey worries me, and when I pull up at the lake, I can't look at her. I get out of the car and leave her in the passenger seat. The veil of vexation starts to lift, and I glance back at Layla, who's paled further as she stays seated in the car.

I'm walking back to her. Each step I take has her breathing growing more irregular. I pull open her door.

"Those three days... Where were you?" My patience snaps. "Who's the boy?"

Layla closes her eyes, and I'm ready to reach in and shake her when they flutter open.

"I had some bad news and needed time off." Her voice shakes only slightly, and she unclips her seat belt. I wasn't aware she had put it on. "Can I get out, please?"

I'm crowding her, but I step back and let her out.

Once she stands outside the door, she speaks. "Nelson died. I'm not sure you heard." Sadness floods her blue eyes.

I take a step away from her and watch her from the corner of my eye. "How?" My heart beats wildly.

She wraps her arms around her waist. "I don't know. They wouldn't tell me."

Bile bubbles in my stomach, and I take another step away from Layla.

My father's words about the boy make me feel sick. He knew. He knew Nelson died and didn't tell me.

"Jay." Layla steps closer to me, reaching out like she's ready to offer me her condolences.

"Don't fucking touch me."

She jerks back; her features tighten before she explodes. "Why do you hate me? What have I done?" Her voice shakes, and she points a finger at me. "I'm sorry. I'm sorry you had to keep protecting me. I'm sorry I destroyed your life." Her lip trembles, and she battles the pain that fills her eyes. "I am so sorry, Jared."

"Shut the fuck up." I can't breathe.

"You left me." Her words break and crack.

"I said shut up," I growl.

She doesn't hear me, but I start to walk away from her, from my past, from the emotions that are clawing at me. I keep walking until I reach the end of the pier.

"I searched for you." Her angry words are hurled at my back. "You leaving destroyed me."

I spin around and face her.

"I..." Her mouth opens and closes, but not one tear that glazes her eyes has escaped. "Jared." She says my name so sweetly, and it undoes me.

I clear the distance and slam my mouth down on hers. She doesn't respond as I taste desperation and peanut butter. I break the one-sided kiss abruptly.

"You were eating peanut butter sandwiches with that little prick?"

Her tongue flicks out and licks her lips. My brain is still analyzing how it felt to kiss her. Fucking amazing. Her lips are softer than they look, warmer. Her scent has stolen my ability to smell anything else. Nothing can compete with the scent of Layla.

"He offered me one."

My temper flares, and my fingers grip her. She spins so easily in my hands as I face her toward the lake.

"Jared, I can't swim!" she screams as I push her into the lake.

I know.

CHAPTER TWELVE

LAYLA

WATER GUSHES OVER MY head. The last image I have burned into my brain is Jared standing on the edge of the pier with a perplexed look on his striking face. The world turns to green and brown as the lake swallows me whole. Pain burns my lungs, pain that isn't just from being oxygen deprived. Betrayal is a new kind of pain as my brain keeps repeating on a loop that Jared pushed me into the lake with the knowledge that I can't swim.

My arms and legs kick out. My thoughts are not with the action, but I'm aware of the flailing limbs that try to erase the growing distance between me and the surface. The world shatters as something breaks the surface and zooms toward me. I can't see through the murky water as an arm circles my waist, and we're tearing toward the surface. Light glitters off the rising water, and just as my lungs burn for what feels like the final time, the water snaps and bends, and I'm staring at the sky as I gasp for air.

"Slowly. You don't want to choke."

Through the veil of fear and sheer panic, I glance down at Jared, who holds me solidly against his chest with one arm. The other arm moves in my peripheral vision, keeping us afloat.

"In through the nose, out through the mouth." He speaks with a slight smile.

I hate him at this moment, but I'm drawn to the old habit we established for calming me down.

"Take a larger one. Let it fill your belly," Jared says, and my breathing evens out as a new type of hurt digs its talons into me. At this stage, Jared would tickle my stomach, and I would laugh instead of cry, and the crisis would be over.

"Feel it down to your toes," he continues.

I shake my head as my throat and eyes burn. "Stop."

The slight smile he wore disappears, and he continues to keep us afloat in the middle of the lake. Jared hasn't looked away from me, and his arm around my waist is a promise that I'm going nowhere.

His gaze drops to my lips, and more confusion floods my system. Why did he kiss me when he clearly hates me?

I focus on the pier that seems far away. "Take me back to the shore."

"No." Jared's tone draws my attention back to him. "I don't want you around that boy anymore."

I don't ask who. I know who. The one he dragged me away from. But I don't understand why. A breeze dances on the surface of the lake. The water shivers under the caress, and I lean in closer to Jared's solid chest.

I'm aware of how solid, how big, how different he is.

He's a man.

"Fine. Take me back to shore."

His lip twitches, and he leans out so I have to lie across his torso as he swims closer to the pier but not the whole way. He stops and straightens up. His hand pulls me closer, tightening around my waist.

My fingers dig into his wide shoulders. "You knew I couldn't swim." I allow the hurt to pour into my words.

Jared doesn't flinch or wear a look of guilt that anyone else would. His shoulders lift under my touch. "I wouldn't have let you drown."

"You're my fucking hero." The angry words lash out.

They don't cut Jared at all. In fact, they tickle him as he barks out a deep laugh that twists my core.

His laughter dies, and something dark passes his gaze and deepens the brown to a startling black. He dips his head, and I think he's going to kiss me again. He passes my lips, his cheek pressed against mine, and I swear he inhales. Shivers break out across my skin and find their way throughout my body.

"Keep kicking your legs, Layla." His whispered words have me kicking again, and it's funny how my legs move at the same speed as his. We are in sync with each other.

His closeness is doing something funny to my heart, and he still has his face buried in my neck as he sniffs me.

"When did you learn to swim?" I ask. It's what breaks him away from my aching flesh, and he's dragging us back to the pier. The moment he reaches the dock, he turns to me, and I'm airborne as he pushes me up with one arm. I grip the edge and haul myself up. Water spills out on the wood, and before I have a second to process anything, Jared joins me. His T-shirt is plastered to his chest. I spot a chain around his neck; it's not the first time I've noticed it.

"I learned to swim after my father found me." Jared's words are spoken as his gaze travels across my blouse.

Looking down is so pointless. The fabric is glued to my body, and nothing is covered. My cheeks blaze, and when I glance back up at Jared, I don't know what I expect, but his anger isn't it. "I made sure I eliminated every weakness I had."

His large hand that I stare down at is another reminder of how much bigger he is. I swallow more confusion and loss as I look back up at him. "You were never weak to me, Jared," I admit as my vision blurs. Words bubble up and pop before I get to tell him what he meant to me.

He's standing, and I'm being dragged to my feet. "Everyone and everything was stronger than you, Layla. So nothing would seem weak to you." His words are driven with each step we take to his car.

I was weak then, and I still am now. I feel so small as he releases me and moves to the trunk of his car. He returns with an oversized letterman's jacket.

I take it from him, but I can't look at him right now. The old Jared would never say such a thing. He steps closer and reaches out; his hand burns my flesh as he tilts my head back. I swallow so much loss that it's choking me. He's here in front of me, but he's not. My own brain can't seem to process all the emotions that speed through me.

Jared's transfixed on me. His lips move, and his eyes soften. I can almost imagine that he's ready to take back his words. Maybe he wants to apologize for pushing me into the lake. Maybe he wants to tell me he missed me too.

"That boy, Lucas, is only at Kingscourt on my goodwill. I can take it back anytime I want and have him removed." Jared's fingers tighten on my jawline. "You understand?"

It takes my brain a moment to catch up with our conversation. How did we get back to Lucas? Why did he care about Lucas?

"He's harmless—" I start, but Jared's fingers trail up and press firmly against my lips, cutting off my words.

"You will have lunch with me each day at school." He steps away after issuing his bizarre demand. "Get out of those wet clothes." He walks a few feet away and stops, keeping his back to me.

I don't hesitate and start to peel off the wet clothes. The material clings to my body, but I manage to get the shirt over my head. I don't remove my bra before wrapping Jared's jacket across my cold flesh. I could wrap it twice if I wanted to. When I glance up, Jared is facing me. He grips the bottom of his T-shirt and pulls it off over his head. My heart dances wildly in my chest. His body speaks of hours at a gym, his physique in peak condition.

Why did my mind think that all that muscle was created as a product of his childhood, our childhood? My focus is snagged on the chain that hangs around his neck. On the end is a key. I want to ask about it.

Jared throws the T-shirt into the trunk before closing it. He doesn't walk around to the driver's side but returns to me looking ridiculously handsome, with water dripping down his chest from his darkened hair. I get another look at the key before he speaks.

"Trousers too, Layla."

My cheeks heat against the cold. Jared's eyes light up as he takes another large step toward me. He grips the band of his trousers, "I mean, I can take mine off first if it makes you more comfortable."

The teasing in his voice has me almost choking on the pooling saliva in my mouth. "No. Don't. And don't you have a girlfriend?" I say, sounding as jealous as I feel.

I hear his soft laugh as he walks around to the driver's side. I kick off my boots, and a small stream of water pours out beside the tire of the car. I check the pockets of my trousers first and am surprised to find my car keys still there. I take out the key and peel my trousers off, dragging them down they burn my skin, but once I have them off, I stripe off my socks too. The window rolls down.

"I don't have a girlfriend." There's no humor in Jared's voice now.

I hate how happy that makes me feel. "My clothes?" I ask as I gather them off the ground so he can't see the truth in my face that the news makes me happy.

"Throw them in the back."

I do as Jared says before sliding into the front seat. The leather isn't cold but heated under my bottom. I don't look at Jared as I buckle in, and slip the car keys into my pocket. Once I'm done, and we haven't moved, I take a peek at him.

His focus is on my leg. My scarred leg. I'm tempted to tuck it under me. The scar is a reminder of the worst day of my life.

"I'd never heard anyone scream like that." His words are low and haunted.

When I look at Jared, he takes a gulp of air. His hands crumble on his knees as he stares at my leg. The dark ink band around his wrist is another part of him I'm curious about. Why did he get that tattoo?

"I want to know everything," he says, and our gazes crash again. This time, my heart stalls before galloping.

Jared shifts and rests his chin in his hand, two fingers covering his mouth. The intensity in his eyes burns my soul. I swallow all the emotions and clear my throat. I'm not ready to relive that night, but looking at the tension in Jared's shoulders and how still he is, I know this is important to him.

"I was taken straight to the hospital." My voice sounds so weak, and I clear my throat again.

Jared shifts closer to me, and I'm momentarily frozen solid before warmth rushes through my body and thaws the coldness. Jared slowly and carefully takes my hand in his, and I'm dumbfounded as I stare at his tanned one entwining with my small, pale one. A part of me knows our holding hands isn't right, not when Jared has a girlfriend. Yet, I don't pull away. He said he doesn't have one, but Alex seems to believe they're together.

"I had third-degree burns and some nerve damage." My heart jumps with how he's looking at me. His brows furrow, his hand still covering his mouth but tighter. "I'm so sorry." His voice is soft, which doesn't match the hardness of his posture right now.

I'm shaking my head as he speaks the words. "You saved me," I say, squeezing the hand that still holds mine. His thumb moves lazily in a circular motion, and he closes his eyes, letting out a breath. My stomach flounders from each small touch.

Get a grip.

Jared finally opens his eyes. "Keep going." He doesn't sound sure, but a soft tug of my hand has me nodding.

"I also had a fractured leg from the fall. But the worst—" I pause while taking a sip of air as if it's a painkiller. Why is this so hard?

"You can tell me." Jared's voice seems deeper now; his low words have me glancing at him.

"They had to rebreak two previous breaks that never set correctly."

Jared's nostrils flare, and he lets go of my hand.

Heat burns my cheeks. "I'm sorry," I say quickly while he rubs his face.

At my words, his head shoots up. "I'm not mad at you, Layla."

God, why did he sound so angry, then?

He's beside me before I can blink. My heart races as his arm brushes mine. The heat from his naked torso touches my flesh. The position is so intimate.

"I'm mad because I should have reported it a long time ago. I should have stopped it." He ducks his head, not allowing me to see his face, his forehead so close to mine.

"Jared. Look at me," I tell him. He does. "You were just a child, just like me. Please, it hurts my heart to see you blame yourself." My phrase 'hurts my heart' wrestles a smile out of him, and I knew it would. I used to tell him this all the time if he wouldn't dance with me or read me a bedtime story. It was the line that got him every time.

He takes my hand once again, his touch soft, but the violence in his eyes has me wanting to stop.

"What happened next?"

I'm shaking my head.

"What happened next?" Anger snakes and courses through his words.

I skip a lot, as I can see I'm agitating him, so I skip to the happily ever after. I can't bear the way he's looking at me right now.

"They got a counselor for me—Evelyn. She spent weeks listening to me and finally let me meet her husband, Carl. They took me in." I can't stop the smile as I remember that moment Evelyn told me she was taking me home. *Home* was so foreign to me, but I could tell that this time, things would be different, and they were.

Jared does the most bizarre thing. His lips turn up, and it's a real smile. Dimples that I haven't seen in years make an appearance. My chest tightens, and I have to look away before I crack and split in front of him. It's all too much.

"I asked for you, but no one knew anything." Looking up at Jared, I can see my own pain reflected in his eyes. Suddenly, I'm in his arms. My head rests against his chest. The frantic pounding of his heart fills my ear.

No words are spoken between us as we hold each other. It's a past that doesn't deserve a place in the future, yet it seems to have wormed its way in after being buried for seven years.

Jared pulls back. The loss of his arms and warmth has me looking up at him. He no longer appears happy as he moves back fully into his seat.

"Everything turned out fine for you." His words are hollow.

I get an empty feeling in the pit of my stomach as I watch him transform from Jared into Jay in a matter of seconds.

I can feel the coldness in the air and almost taste it as he drives away from the lake with too much anger in his tightening fingers.

"What about you?" I ask.

"You already know, Layla." His words are bitter.

"I don't. So tell me."

His sneer confuses me. "Yeah, I got my happy ending too."

I tighten my hands on my lap. Cold water drips from my hair onto the jacket. "Then why don't you sound happy?" I swallow a lump in my throat.

"Because, Layla"—Jared fires me a sideways glance—"you're here."

His words make no sense, yet they hurt so much. My temper flares. "You brought me here. I didn't ask. You dragged me into your car. You pushed me into a lake."

Jared doesn't respond but continues to drive past the campus.

I'm watching as the college disappears in the side window. "I need to get my bag. I need to call Evelyn."

Silence.

"Jared."

That gets a reaction out of him. "My fucking name is Jay."

"Where are we going?"

"To my home," Jared responds, and I get this horrible feeling, like I'm stuck in an alley with someone I don't quite trust.

CHAPTER THIRTEEN

JARED

CREAMY LEGS CATCH MY attention too many fucking times. Having Layla beside me wearing nothing but my jacket makes me want to keep driving so this time with her doesn't end. It's a new kind of torture having her close but not touching her the way I want to. I take another glance in her direction. She's gnawing on her swollen red lip, and my cock hardens in my trousers.

"I don't want to go to your home. I want you to take me back to campus." Her voice is weak, and she won't look at me.

Like fuck am I taking her back. I'm keeping her close because she's the enemy right now. My father said that she knew where I was all this time. Yet she acted too innocent, like stumbling into Kingscourt was just a coincidence.

Each time I close my eyes, I see her sitting with Lucas, sharing a sandwich.

"How did he know about the peanut butter sandwiches?" I grit out.

She takes a sharp inhale. "Lucas?"

I glance at her, not liking his name in her mouth—a mouth I want to kiss, a mouth I want to fuck. I can't answer as anger keeps my lips glued together.

She frowns. "Other people eat peanut butter sandwiches, Jar—Jay."

I grip the steering wheel and take one final look at her legs, which she tries to tug closer to the seat like she can hide them from me. I refocus on the road.

I don't want her to hide. I want every single tiny piece of Layla. I slow down as I near my home. My father isn't here; he's off in London at a meeting, so I'll have the place to myself.

I keep an eye on Layla as we pull up to the white gates. She ducks her head and glances out the front windshield to take in the house. She doesn't say anything as I drive up to the mansion. We wait for a moment as the garage door silently rolls up, and I park in my usual spot, and still, she doesn't speak. Her hand shakes as she unclips her belt. That's the first sign that she's nervous. That is, until she glances in my direction. Her blue eyes pierce the darkness in me; her light burns in the worst kind of way, and I drink in her gaze.

"I would have eaten lunch with you every day, Jay. You just had to ask." Her voice is soft. She pulls down the jacket so the material covers her knees.

"I'm not asking, Layla. I'm telling you." I grin in delight as her cheeks heat. Her blue eyes cloud over, and her lids flutter closed, cutting me off from all kinds of torture.

I get out of the car before I reach across and kiss her again. She hesitates only for a moment before she gets out too. She doesn't follow me immediately but gathers her clothes from the back of the car. "Is there somewhere I can dry these?"

I nod and turn away. She looks terrified. We enter the foyer and William materializes.

"Master Jay." He nods and hands me a piece of paper that I don't open. William acknowledges Layla with a bow. "Miss."

My home holds the most exquisite furnishings. Marble that is carved into statues, painted portraits of my father, and items that my father acquired from far-off lands. But nothing looks as foreign as Layla at this moment. I take a step toward her. A smile springs and steals my frown as I reach for her. I have to pry the clothes from Layla's hands. "I'm not going to steal them," I tease.

She doesn't smile, but color seeps beautifully into her cheeks, and instead of stepping away from her, I reach up and touch her pink cheek. The heat radiates into my hand and fills me up.

I must still be smiling, because her eyes are smiling at me.

William clears his throat.

The coldness returns as I remove my hand from Layla and pass William the wet pile of clothes. "Can you dry these, please?"

"Yes, Master Jay." William leaves, and I turn to find Layla glancing around. I reach out, and she startles as my fingers graze hers. I should stop, but I entwine our fingers together. Her blue eyes zero in on our hands, and I give her a tug, leading her toward the stairs. I feel the strain on my hand as she hesitates, but it's too late for that. I pull her easily, and we climb the two flights of stairs until we stop at the third floor.

"Can I use a phone?" The pulse flickers wildly in her neck.

"Who do you want to ring? The Gardaí?" I ask and release her hand.

Layla frowns. "Evelyn. My phone's at school. I'm sure she has called me and is worried." Layla folds her arms across her chest.

Even in my letter jacket and nothing else, she's the most beautifully destructive thing I have ever seen.

"You're not good for me." I take a step closer to her. "You shouldn't be here," I say as I tilt her head back using the tip of my fingers under her chin. Bringing her here was a bad idea.

"I agree," Layla bites out, but her gaze lands on my lips.

I let them rise, and she shivers before looking up to mine. "Take me home."

Home. Is that what she's calling it?

I release her and walk away, entering the sitting area. I open a drawer and power on one of my spare phones. The other one got lost in the lake. Once it powers up, I turn to find Layla standing close to me. She's checking me out. I hold out the phone. She reaches out, and I pull it back, forcing her to look at me.

"You ring only Evelyn," I warn.

She doesn't answer, and I keep the phone held away from her. The want to touch Layla has me stepping closer. She cowers in front of me. I don't want her to cower.

"Make your call." I push the phone into Layla's hand and leave her.

"Hi, have you been trying to call me?" Her voice shakes, and I pause in the hall. Why is she afraid? Is Evelyn hurting her?

"I'm sorry. I left my bag in class." Her words are stronger. I can't hear the voice on the other end of the phone. "No. Ashley, my friend, invited me to her house to study."

Of course, she won't mention me.

I don't shower but change into a fresh pair of jogging pants and a black T-shirt. I towel dry my hair and return to Layla. She's standing where I left her, the phone still clutched in her hand. I want to know what she's thinking. When she glances up at me, defiance flashes in her eyes, and I wonder if she rang the Gardaí, saying I kidnapped her. I clear the space and swipe the phone from her hand. I flick open the dial log and can only see one number.

I look at Layla. I've seen that look in her eyes before. The defiance is fucking prepossessing.

"Remember when you pushed Ronnie's doll pram down the stairs?"

Her eyes light up, and she unfolds her arms from across her chest. The jacket gaps slightly, and I see a glimpse of white flesh. My heart thumps, my cock grows instantly, and the memory evaporates as I take a small step closer to her.

"It was the best feeling ever." She smiles, and I'm back there with her again.

My lips drag up. "It hit every step with a bang." One push sent the pram sailing down the stairs. The rattles sound distant as I recall the memory. I remember the satisfaction in Layla's eyes that day; they shone with the defiance I saw only moments ago.

I laugh. "It was the ugliest pram."

Layla folds her arms across her chest, dragging the jacket back into place, hiding all that tempting skin. "Blue. The doll pram was like an egg blue velvet material. It was her pride and joy. Her father had bought it for her, and she said it was mine. Like I wanted anything from her." The smile melts off Layla's face.

I take a step back as her face tightens.

When I left Layla that day, I was smiling. Bert and Ronnie were out, and no one would know what she had done. The pram showed no signs of damage.

"How did you get it back upstairs?" I ask as I think back. I had left to go hang out with Fintan and Keith.

Layla drops her gaze. "I didn't. Ronnie did."

I dip my head to make Layla look at me, but she won't. "Ronnie wasn't there." Is this another lie? Just like the one she was telling me, pretending she didn't know where I was all these years. Like the lie she just told Evelyn, saying she was at Ashley's.

Layla finally looks at me. "She was asleep in the conservatory. The noise must have woken her. You had just left when she arrived in the hall."

I'm shaking my head. "She and Bert were gone. I remember."

"She was there. I remember that day clearly." Layla unfolds her arms, showing me some skin again. Is she doing it on purpose, trying to distract me? "I want to go home."

"No." I'm not ready for her to leave yet.

"You can't stop me." Layla spins, and I see the panic in her eyes.

"I mean, you can't leave wearing only my jacket. Your clothes should be dry soon. But I'll get you some fresh clothes while you wait."

She turns back and blinks several times at my logic. "Fine."

I take her to my bedroom. The door at the end of the hall is like a beacon. A warning. What would she think if she saw inside that room? When I glance back at Layla, she's followed my gaze. I'm tempted to reach up and touch the key that dangles around my neck.

"What happened with Ronnie?" I ask as I enter my bedroom. I take a moment to look at Layla standing close to my bed. How many times have I pictured her here—lying on my bed while I fuck her? I switch on the light in the closet and enter, getting a T-shirt for her. When I step back into my room, she's glancing around, and I wonder if she ever fantasizes about me the way I have obsessed over her all these years.

I walk to her, and she swallows. "Tell me what happened." I keep the T-shirt out of her reach.

"It doesn't matter, Jar—Jay," she bites out.

It fucking matters a lot. Every single detail about her existence matters.

I don't speak but glare at her, and it does the trick.

"I ran upstairs into my room, and she followed me. She was beyond angry." Layla's blue eyes darken. "I pressed myself against the wardrobe. I just knew I had really messed up. She didn't slow down when she entered the room. She slapped me across the face." Layla takes in a large breath. "I kept waiting for her to stop, but with each slap, I soon realized she wouldn't. So I screamed."

My fingers tighten around the fabric in my hand. A throb starts in my gut as I watch her torture herself with each word I make her relive.

"I didn't stop screaming until she was dragged off me. I've never seen Bert so angry." She blinks several times, and when I move closer, she doesn't even notice.

"He was fucking livid. She was afraid of him. Really afraid. Like the fear we felt." Layla peeks at me then. "He forced her to stare at me, and he was shouting at her to look at my face. That she had marked me."

Layla breathes heavily again, and it's like she's stepping out of the memory.

How had I not noticed that her face was marked? I noticed everything about Layla.

"You didn't look hurt the next day," I say, and I'm touching her cheek. She flinches under my touch but settles at a second.

"Bert had placed cold washcloths on my face that whole evening and night."

My gut twists painfully, and my heart starts to hammer. My brain tries to force thoughts I don't want, and I can't take much more of them. I grip Layla by the back of the neck and drag her face to mine. Her eyes widen as our noses touch. "I've dreamt of fucking you," I confess.

She tries to pull herself out of my hand, and I clamp down on her neck. "In the most delicious ways," I continue.

She pales further, and it isn't my desired effect. I just want to speak my truths that cover up other truths. I inhale her openly, not shying away from how I must appear.

She whimpers, and the hairs rise on the back of my neck.

"I would never hurt you," I whisper against her lips. They shake before I press mine against hers. The kiss is soft, but my thoughts are disturbed. Fucking her is all I want, but I keep my hand on her neck to keep us rooted to the spot so I don't force her back onto the bed. So I don't take every single piece of Layla for myself.

Her mouth doesn't move under mine, not even when my teeth graze her lips or when my tongue prods against her mouth. After a few torturous moments, she turns her head away from me. Her breaths are fast and hard, and I'm staring at her pink cheeks. I press a hard kiss against her face before I release her.

She won't look at me, but I'm not leaving until she does.

I hold out the T-shirt. "You need to change."

She shakes her head. "No, thank you. I'll wait for my clothes."

"You can wait in my bedroom if you want."

Her head snaps up toward me, and I grin.

"I'd prefer to wait in the living room."

I give a sweeping gesture toward the door, and she scurries past me. Her long legs move fast, and I'm snagged on her scar again.

We enter the living room, and her clothes are folded on the chair. I didn't hear William enter. Layla doesn't miss a beat but starts to drag on her trousers, then her socks. Her shirt is in the trunk of my car. I walk to her and reach around. She freezes as I place my T-shirt on the arm of the chair.

"I'll give you a moment," I say, and I don't turn away as she shrugs out of the jacket. Her skin is flawless, her back begging to be touched. I can imagine running my hand down her spine, making her bend over. My cock grows quickly, and I turn away from her.

"Thank you." Her voice has me turning around.

My T-shirt falls down to her knees, the material swallowing her up. My jacket hangs across the arm of the chair. Layla pulls on her boots, which can't be dry. "I'm ready to go."

"I'm not ready to let you go."

She tilts her head. "Please, Jay."

CHAPTER FOURTEEN

LAYLA

AIR IS RARER THAN gold dust right now. I'm struggling to find enough to satisfy my lungs as Jared towers over me. He's larger than life. He's angrier than a storm. He has a savage beauty about him that makes being in his presence hard to bear.

Jared steps back to the chair and gathers up his jacket. I'm frozen to the spot as he returns, and with such a tenderness that sings to the most humane part of me, he drapes the coat over my shoulders, and my pain wants to howl his name.

"Let's go." His words are hollow, and the echo of them has my pain burning up faster than dry paper. I follow him quickly out of the mansion. Taking snapshots in my mind of the architecture that under normal circumstances I would admire, my mind reels. I can't believe this is where he lives. It appears that Jared has everything. Appearances can be and are deceiving, though. I've never seen another human so empty at times.

I shiver and wrap my arms around my waist as I follow Jared into the garage. He unlocks the car and slides into the driver's seat. When he looks up at me, my heart thumps. Walking around the car makes me aware of how I'm holding myself, how I'm walking, as his gaze soaks in everything about me. I get in and focus on buckling the belt.

The car hums under us as Jared reverses out of the garage. He's gone silent, and I don't want his silence right now. His confession about thinking about fucking me threw me for a loop. I have no idea how to feel or what to make of his honesty. Falling in love with Jared wouldn't be good for my heart. Falling in love with Jay would be so easy but so dangerous. I don't think the damage would be just my heart, but my mind, my body, even my soul. My traitorous heart thumps away in my chest as I replay his words.

We pull up to campus, and now I'm the one who's not ready to go. I'm confused, and some part of me wants Jared for a moment so we can figure this out. Jared would be levelheaded about this. Jay is too unpredictable.

"Jared..." I start the moment the car stops. He isn't facing me, but the words get lost as a shadow looms over the passenger side before moving away.

Jared rolls down his window as Chester approaches his door.

"Hey, bro." Chester gives me a fleeting glance.

"What's going on?"

Jared nods before hitting Chester's outstretched hands—first a slap, then a back slap, then bumping fists. "Nothing much. What are you doing here?"

This time, Chester looks at me while raising his head. "What's up?"

My mind falters. *What's up?* My mouth is dry as I force myself not to get up and run. I just nod back.

"I was looking for you." Chester grins at Jared.

Is Jared in some kind of trouble? I crumble internally.

"You could have called me." Jared's fingers dance across the doorframe as he speaks.

"I did, brother. I got no answer," Chester says, his glance flickering to me again.

Another car pulls into the parking lot, and I can't make out the driver. Only their profile as the daylight is starting to fade.

Unbuckling my belt slowly, I try to be quiet so I don't draw attention to myself until I'm ready to leave. "I'd better go." I finally look at Jared to find him studying me.

"I'll drop you home."

Chester is taking us in, and shivers snake across my skin. I rub the back of my neck. "I'm good." I need to leave.

My heart palpitates.

"Go get your bag. I said I'll drop you home." Jared leans forward, his hands clasped together, his gaze intense.

"Jay, my car is right there. There is no need." He's being overbearing right now, and with Chester watching me too, I just want to get away from them.

"I'll wait here until you're in your car."

I glare at Jared. "What, you think someone might kidnap me?" I snap at how ridiculous he's being.

His lips twitch, but they don't form into a full smile. He brushes dark locks off his forehead.

"Nice seeing you, Layla." Chester's voice has my shoulders curling in, and I don't look back as I make my way to my car.

My nerves are shot, and I have no idea how I feel about everything that just transpired. From being dumped in the lake, to his crude words about fucking me, all the way to that kiss.

When we were younger, Jared held my hand as we walked to the shops or to go to his hangout spot with the guys. I never thought anything of his nearness to me, but now that we're older, it feels so much different. The moment I slide into the car, I scoop out my phone and see four missed calls from Evelyn. I don't look over to where Jared's car had been parked. My pulse spikes as I imagine him walking toward me, ready to force me back into his car. I hit the locks on the doors.

This is Jared, I remind myself. So why am I having such a hard time with my feelings toward him? My mind seems to race at a million miles an hour. How can anyone evoke so many different emotions in someone?

The ding of my phone niggles at my nerves. I click the yellow open icon, and my body stills. It's a text from Jared.

Why are you sitting in your car?

I glance around me. He's leaning against his car with his hands deep in his pockets. His eyes clash with mine, and I shiver. The chill has nothing to do with the weather. He doesn't move a muscle.

My fingers move quickly over my phone. **I'm thinking** I type quickly before looking at him in the rearview mirror. He has his phone out and is typing.

About what? His response is one I expect. My answer and decision are already made. I was weak then, but I am strong now.

You. I watch Jared as I hit send. His brows drag down, and he glances up at me from under thick, dark lashes. Stuffing his phone into his pocket, he pushes off the hood of his car and starts walking toward mine.

I peel my hands off the steering wheel and unlock the passenger door to let him in.

The smell of his cologne immediately fills the small space. He shifts, taking his phone out and setting the slick black device on the dash before twisting his body so he can face me.

"Talk to me."

I chew my lip, trying to think of the best way to phrase this.

"Don't think. You always overthink everything. Just talk." The command from Jared startles me. I can't read any expression on his face, but I'm familiar with his tone. He's worried.

"You haven't said anything about Nelson." It's my turn to be perturbed. I wasn't exactly sure where that came from, but that's what pops out of my mouth.

Jared glances away, his hand going to his phone. He picks it up and taps the device on his knee as he speaks. "What's there to say? He's dead."

My shoulders tense. This isn't the Jared I remember. Jared, who stood up to the bullies and the monsters. Jared, who took on the world with his ten-year-old fists. Jared, who protected all of us, including Nelson.

I swallow the emotion that swells inside me. "You could say how you feel about it, maybe."

He works his jaw, his focus out the window. "How do you feel about it, Layla?" he asks while glancing at me.

"Upset, of course."

Jared's gaze is hooded, and I'm not sure what he's thinking. A knock on the window drags a startled cry from me. He rolls down the window to Chester.

"Didn't mean to frighten you," Chester says, his words heavy with so much more. Jared continues to tap his phone on his knee.

"That's okay," I manage to get out between dry lips.

"Just give me a minute," Jared says, and Chester nods at him before standing up and out of my view.

"No problem, bro," Chester responds as Jared rolls up the window.

My brows rise as Jared turns to me. I have so many questions to ask him, especially about Chester. But now isn't the time.

Rubbing his hands on his jeans before scratching his jaw, he faces me once again. "When can I meet Evelyn and Carl?"

Coldness seeps into my skin before a blast of heat burns my blood. I look away this time, my hands going to the steering wheel. "I... I don't know." I glance at him.

He sits stiffly. Can he hear the rest of that statement? The part where I haven't told them about finding him. Also, if this were Jared, I would have him at our dinner table, but Jay? That's the part I'm not sure about.

Jared scratches his jaw again, where a shadow of new growth is forming. I didn't notice it before. "I've got to go. But I'll text later."

I'm nodding when the smell of his cologne intensifies as he leans in and kisses me softly on the cheek. Our gazes collide when he leans away, but neither of us says anything.

"I've got to go," he repeats.

"Yeah," I say as he climbs out of my car. Once the door closes, my whole body sags.

***

After pulling into the drive, I sit in my car for a few moments. I'm not sure what's eating at me more—the fact that I lied to Evelyn and Carl about Jared, or that I haven't told Jared the truth about not telling them about him. Or maybe the fact that Jared pushed me into a lake. Or that he has looked at me with hate more times than I can count.

Carl comes out of the house as I close the car door. I clutch my bag tightly.

"Is everything okay?" I ask as Carl nears.

He smiles faintly. "Yeah, I just have to go to work. Are you okay?"

My pulse picks up. "Yeah, just tired."

Carl doesn't say anything, but his eyes narrow slightly. "Evelyn is inside if you need to talk." He squeezes my shoulder while his thick brows rise. "But work can wait if you need me?"

His words cause a heaviness in my chest. Lying to them is wrong. They've taken me into their home and have always maintained an open relationship with me. I've never been dishonest with them before.

"No. Thanks, Carl. Honestly, nothing's wrong. I'm just tired." After another squeeze of my shoulder and a promise that I can call him if I change my mind, I go inside with my head hanging. I feel like such a terrible person. After dumping my bag in the hall, I enter the kitchen, having decided to tell Evelyn the truth. She has her back to me as she shuffles potatoes on the baking tray. The smell would typically cause my mouth to water, but not now. The warmth of the kitchen has me stripping off Jared's jacket. I pause as I place it on the back of the chair. I'd forgotten about his clothes. Evelyn glances over at me quickly while pushing the tray back into the oven.

"Oh, you're just in time. It's nearly ready," Evelyn says while closing the door. Her long silver sweater and tan leggings fit her perfectly. She really is a beautiful-looking woman. Pushing her glasses up into her hair, she fully faces me. Her brows pull down, and she gives me nearly the identical look that Carl gave me.

"Is there something bothering you?" She picks up a cloth while moving around the island to sit beside me. I join my hands together and rest them on the table to stop myself from fidgeting. The need to touch my face or neck has me considering sitting on my hands. The heat coming from the oven is starting to make the room uncomfortable. Evelyn glances at my hands. Immediately, I loosen my grip.

"Is that a man's T-shirt you're wearing?" More worry worms its way into Evelyn's eyes.

"I found Jared." It comes out in one rushed breath.

Evelyn sits back slightly in her chair. Others might not have noticed it—the movement is that slight. But I've spent a lot of time being counseled by Evelyn, and this tells me she's shocked but is processing the knowledge. When I spoke about Bert and all he made me suffer, she would listen and talk me through my feelings. Most of the time, it frustrated the crap out of me. I just wanted to tell my story, not zone in on feelings. In my head, I thought Evelyn was stupid. How could she not know I was angry and hurt?

But as I put my emotions under the microscope, I began to see something different. My feelings of anger were directed at myself for allowing Bert to catch me off guard. Or for not speaking up when he asked a question. That's when I started paying closer attention to my emotions. When I could tell Evelyn what I was feeling, she would always tap her notepad or folder with two fingers. I didn't think she knew what she was doing at the time. It was her 'tell' that let me know she was proud. At times when I spoke of Ronnie, Evelyn would sit back ever so slightly. She would listen, and it would take her a few moments to respond. She was gathering her thoughts, just like she is now.

"You must have been relieved."

That isn't the response I expected. I nod. "I was shocked." I let out a small breath along with a shaky smile, allowing myself to really feel the happiness of finding Jared alive.

Evelyn smiles faintly. "I can only imagine. You must have been overwhelmed."

"I'm still processing it," I tell Evelyn.

Tapping the table with two fingers briefly, she smiles. "I'm happy for you, Layla."

I loosen the grip on my hands, and a smile takes over my face. "Thanks, Evelyn. I... He's... different now. But still the same. You know?" I chew my lip, hoping what I'm saying makes sense. How could it? She didn't know him then. She doesn't even know him now.

"It's been seven years. That's a long time. I'm sure he's feeling the same about you as you are about him."

My face burns. I don't think Evelyn would be happy to know how Jared feels about me now. I'm honestly not sure what Jared feels when he sees me. A reminder of a past he'd rather forget?

Evelyn wipes the table with the cloth; I can tell she's choosing her next words carefully.

"I'm happy you found him, but Jared is from your past. One that gave you a lot of heartache. I just worry that his reappearing will bring your past back up. You've come such a long way, Layla. I would hate to think anything would set you back."

I react like a goldfish: my mouth repeatedly opens and closes. I have so much I want to say to that. Evelyn's hands cover mine now.

"I'm underestimating you. I know what he meant to you. How he basically kept you alive. I'm not going to lie. I worry about you." Evelyn brushes my hair back from my forehead—a motherly gesture that always causes a pang in my chest, though I've never told her that. She pauses, looking me in the eye, a smile on her face. "I will always worry about you."

"Thank you," I say, feeling lighter, but so tired. A final pat to my hand and Evelyn gets up.

"I better take out the potatoes and chicken, or we won't have anything to eat."

I watch Evelyn move around the kitchen. She isn't moving as freely as she usually does, but I don't expect her to take this news with smiles and hugs. I knew it would be a struggle for all of us. My phone dings, and I slip the device out of my bag.

You will have lunch with me tomorrow.

My pulse starts to pick up as I stare at the message. Time passes, though I'm not sure how long. I just now notice the piping hot plate of food in front of me and that Evelyn sits across from me.

"Is it Kieran?" The hope in her voice shatters my guilt-free ride. I lied about Kieran too. Something says I shouldn't tell her yet. Telling her about Jared is enough; I'll deal with Kieran another time.

"It's Jared." It feels nice to be honest again. Lying is way too much work.

Evelyn leans back in her chair slightly. I don't rush her but let her fight whatever internal debate she's clearly having. The pause feels like it goes on forever.

"You never told me where you found him." If my guilt-free ride shattered earlier, it's squashed into oblivion now.

Don't lie, Layla. Just tell the truth and face the consequences.

"Kingscourt College. He goes there also." I chew my lip.
Please don't ask for a timeline.

I don't want to let Evelyn down. She's been so good to me. I pray for this one small detail to be overlooked, and guess what?

It is.

CHAPTER FIFTEEN

LAYLA

I LIE IN BED that night, staring at the ceiling. Carl comes home from work, and I wring my hands as I listen to his and Evelyn's hushed voices. Carl's is raised slightly, but I still can't understand what he's saying. A part of me wants to leave my cozy double bed and try to listen in on their conversation, but the sensible and tired part of me keeps me in bed. Their discussion lulls for a while, and I start to drift off. The ping of my phone has me pushing the lavender duvet off me as I reach for it on the side table.

Don't make me come looking for you.

That one sentence from Jared plays havoc with my emotions. I want to pause them and place them under the microscope like Evelyn had taught me, but I'm drained. Instead, I text back quickly, not doubting his threat.

I'll have lunch with you tomorrow. I hit send before I can think any more about him. I don't even get the phone put back down when it pings again.

That was a given. See you tomorrow, Layla.

I stare at his message. Footsteps on the stairs have me putting the phone down and pulling the duvet up to my neck. I don't want to have a conversation with Carl about Jared. My door opens slightly, and I release the death grip I have on the quilt. I can picture Carl raised up on his toes, trying to see me under the mountains of blankets. My breathing sounds so heavy and fast, and I try to even it out.

"Night, Layla." Carl's words have me crashing and burning.

"Night, Carl," I whisper back, unable to keep up the pretense. As he turns on my bedroom light, the harsh brightness burns my eyes, and I close them tightly.

"I thought you were asleep."

Okay, so we're doing this now. "Not yet." I sit up and rub my eyes.

The heaviness of his gaze and the dark circles indicate just how tired he is. "So you found Jared?"

I nod, stopping myself from clutching the blanket.

"When can we meet him?"

That, I didn't expect. "Meet him?" I say back, not sure how I feel about this.

"Yes. As in, he comes over for dinner, and we all chat." Carl smiles now while squeezing my knee through the quilt.

"Yeah, we can do that. I'll ask him."

Carl jerks his head while standing. "Great." He seems really happy. When he flips off my light, I flop back down into my pillows.

"Good night, Layla," Carl says before closing the door.

"Night, Carl," I respond, even as my mind reels. They want to meet Jared. They don't want to meet Jay, but Jared. I need him to be Jared when he comes here. Jared *is* Jay. He's just different. I toss and turn until I try to settle my mind with memories.

The grass brushes my shoulders. The daisies give life to the greenery springing up and overtaking an area. Walking with my arms stretched out, I let my fingers thread through the grass. The earth dips beneath me when we're close to our destination.

"Why did she have to come? She always slows us down."

I roll my eyes at Ray's stupid words. Jared always takes me with him, even though the other boys complain. He's bigger and stronger than they are, so I'm allowed to come.

"Shut it unless you want me to knock out your teeth," Jared threatens. Nelson and Rocky snigger. The grass falls away, and a barbed-wire fence with a forest beyond comes into view. The forest is our destination. It's where we spend most of our days playing warfare. I don't do much; I stay by the tree and attend to any wounds that the boys get.

"You could make him hold the wire for ten seconds," Nelson says, his grin huge across his face. He's originally from Kenya. His dark skin is something I haven't seen much of, so he always fascinates me.

"Twenty seconds," Rocky says, and Ray holds his hands up, taking a step away from the boys.

"I said I was sorry." I usually don't feel sorry for Ray. He's always moaning about me coming along, but the boys teasing him isn't nice. And we all know the fence is electrified to keep the cattle in the field that we stand in now.

"You sound like a bunch of girls." I step out of the grass, and all heads turn my way. Jared is holding a stick as tall as himself. A grin spreads across his face at my words.

"Layla's right. You do sound like a bunch of girls," Jared declares.

Nelson tuts while he moves closer to the fence that's now within reaching distance. "I'll touch the fence."

"No, you won't." Ray smirks now, the brazenness returning to his stance. His short beige cut-offs showcase his stick-thin legs, which are coated in bruises. I've heard that Mrs. April is mean with her wooden spoon.

"Yes, I will." Nelson doesn't sound so sure anymore. I can see sweat starting to appear on his forehead.

"Oh, for Pete's sake. Jared, tell them to stop." Someone is going to get hurt. Everyone listens to Jared, so he should stop this. His grin grows as he leans with both hands on his stick.

"I'm not their daddy, and if they want to touch the fence, I can't stop them."

I narrow my eyes at Jared, and he laughs, the sound echoing across the fence and into the forest.

Now all I want is for someone to touch the fence so we can stop standing around like a bunch of ninnies.

"I knew you didn't have the stomach," Ray says, as he starts to walk away from us, and I'm glad to follow. I haven't taken a step when Nelson grabs the fence. I scream as his body shakes violently. Ray and Rocky race to him, but no one touches him as he continues to be electrified. Jared drops to the ground as we all stand stunned, watching Nelson.

Will he die?

One thing I've learned is to not touch someone in this situation, because the electricity will pass into your own body and the pain is worse. Jared unlaces his shoes and stands with them on his hands. He's reaching out toward Nelson when Nelson stops shaking, and an odd sound comes from him. I'm ready to puke.

Laughter? Nelson is laughing wildly as he turns to us. "I got you all." I slowly sink into the grass. He was only pretending.

"I knew that," Ray says, but everyone looks a little pale. Jared drops his shoes and punches Nelson in the arm, cutting off his laughter.

"That wasn't funny." Now he points at me. "You scared Layla half to death."

I want to protest and state that everyone was pretty scared, but I know it's pointless. They would all deny it. I stay seated as everyone looks around, pretending to scout for... what? Cows? Jared laces up his battered shoes close to me. The strain on his laces makes me believe they'll snap at any moment. But they don't. Jared glances at me through his long, thick hair.

"You okay?" He reties his hair while waiting for me to answer.

I nod and stand, smoothing down my yellow butterfly dress. It's my favorite. Jared said it's the same color as my hair. The dress is bright yellow, nothing close to my hair, but I thanked him and agreed.

"We're moving out." Jared's command has us all falling in line behind him. I'm directly behind him; he wouldn't have it any other way. No matter where we are, he's always protecting me.

Behind me, Nelson still mocks Ray and Rocky about believing his little trick. "Even Jared knew it was a joke."

I roll my eyes at Jared's back. Jared's their leader, so obviously, he knows when they're joking. The bleeping has me glancing down at my cracked watch that's never worked. I stop walking, bringing the watch closer to my ear. The beeping grows louder. Looking up, Jared is still walking.

"Layla." I squint and see brown eyes, caramel skin, and a recognizable female voice.

"Layla," Evelyn says louder while turning off my alarm.

"I'm up," I say groggily, pushing the blankets back and letting my feet touch the wooden floor. The smell of the forest still lingers in the air. That felt so real. I haven't thought about that day in such a long time. I don't have to ask why I'm dredging up old memories. I know why. Between Nelson's death and Jared's reappearance, old memories are bound to resurface. Even the good ones. That was a good day, even if I didn't know it at the time.

Light streams in as Evelyn pulls back the curtains. "Carl told me he spoke to you last night." I don't have to see Evelyn to know she's smiling; her voice carries the happiness around my room.

"Yeah, he wants to meet Jared," I say, still shaking off the memory of my dream. Evelyn appears in front of me, holding my washing to her chest. "Are you okay, sweetheart?" Her brows pull down with concern.

My toes wiggle against the wooden floor as I shake off the final threads of the memory. "Yeah, just weird dreams. I'm excited and nervous for you guys to meet him."

Evelyn smiles, the crinkles growing around her dark eyes. "Don't be nervous. We promise not to embarrass you."

"I'm not worried about you, Evelyn," I say, smiling.

A small laugh erupts from Evelyn's mouth. "I'll keep Carl in order. Don't worry. Now, come eat breakfast so you're not late for class."

Class. I almost forgot. Evelyn leaves, and I get dressed in a red shirt and black trousers. After braiding my blonde hair over one shoulder, I wash and make my way downstairs. Evelyn has my breakfast ready. I grab a slice of toast off the table while picking up my bag, keys, and Jared's jacket.

"Are you not sitting?" Evelyn's disapproval of eating on the go fills her words.

I kiss her quickly on the cheek. "I'm late, so just this once." I smile while she wipes crumbs off her cheek from where I kissed her.

She calls goodbye as I leave for class.

***

I end up making it just in time. Ashley is waiting for me near the main doors. The moment her gaze settles on me, she unfolds her arms and walks across the hallway to meet me.

"Are you okay? I heard that Jay dragged you into his car. I mean, Sam said he was terrifying." Ashley's head jerks as she speaks.

"I'm okay." I shrug.

. "It's fine. He just wanted to talk," I say.

Ashley looks concerned, and the more I look at her, I notice the dark circles that pull the normal brightness from her eyes. She grips a ballpoint pen and clicks the top down. The click seems loud between us, and she does it again.

"We had some unfinished business to discuss. I'm fine," I reassure her and hate how she still looks at me. "Is everything okay with you, Ashley?" I focus on her thumb that keeps pushing down on the pen top before glancing up at her briefly.

She gives me a tired smile while tilting her head to the side. "Nicco was up a lot last night. He was sleeping when I left this morning. I wanted to climb into his crib and cuddle up beside him."

A small laugh bursts from me, picturing her with her son. "Do you have a picture of him?"

Ashley's eyes light up as she bounces before shifting her notepads to one arm so she can pull her phone out of her pocket. Her fingers move across the screen, and she turns the phone to me. She slides a small image of the cutest baby I've ever seen up on the screen. My heart melts.

"Oh, Ashley, he's so adorable. I want to hug him," I tell her.

Her smile widens. "I know. He brings me so much joy."

He's a miniature version of her. With big brown eyes and a wide smile, his face looks so animated. The little red pajamas cover his tiny but pudgy body.

"But he also wants a lot of attention—sometimes too much." Her smile grows tired as she takes her phone back and pushes it into her pocket.

"If you're ever looking for a babysitter, I'm available." My cheeks heat as I say it. It's stupid; she doesn't know me, and she would hardly trust me with her little baby. "I mean, if you're stuck. Don't feel obliged." I shrug, making a mess of the conversation.

Ashley lowers her gaze. Oh god, she doesn't know how to say no. Heat starts to flow all over my face now.

"That would be great," Ashley says.

My eyes widen with surprise.

"How about tonight?" Ashley is squinting briefly. "Only if that suits. I hate to take you up on your offer so suddenly, but I actually would love a night out, and it so happens I was invited to a party."

"Yes, perfect."

"I'll give you my address later. Is eight okay?" she asks.

"Yep. That's great." I swallow now, a little nervous as I head to class. I've babysat kids before, but it's been a while. A long while.

I settle into my seat and sigh. I don't want the class to end, as it's closing in on lunchtime. I haven't seen Jared, but his promise that we were having lunch together makes my stomach squirm way too much and for lots of different reasons.

***

When I leave class, a shadow looms beside me. I know it's him. I don't even need to look to know.

It's Jared.

The smell of his cologne circles me and crushes my chest until I stop walking. He does too, and I take my first look at him.

My nerves jump and flail. All I see is Jay, who's god-like and angry and waiting for me to say something. I try to find Jared in his eyes so I can calm my frazzled heart.

"Do you remember the electric fence?" My words aren't what I wanted to say, but I don't stop the flow of babble. "The day Nelson pretended to be electrified?"

Jared folds his large arms across his chest. The gray sweater stretches with the movement. The shadow of anger grows, and I can't hold his stare. "What about it?"

I swallow a lump. "Did you really know he was joking?" Why did this matter to me?

Jared unfolds his arms. His gaze dances across my face, and each touch latches on to some fragile part of my being and gives it comfort. "No."

Surprise lifts my lips. "Really?" My question comes out in half a laugh.

One dimple appears on Jared's cheek. "He scared me that day." Jared takes a step closer.

I swallow and focus on his dimple. I want to touch it.

"But I was the leader, so I couldn't show fear. I had to know everything."

"You hid it well." I speak to his chest as the air grows heavy between us.

"You hide things well too."

The wrath in his gaze has me stumbling back into the wall; the sounds of the hallway and people come crashing back. Everyone who passes us stares openly.

Jared steps back, his features becoming indifferent. "It's time for lunch, so I'm here to join you."

One full hour with Jared. I have no idea how I'm going to survive this.

CHAPTER SIXTEEN

JARED

S HE'S NERVOUS. HER GAZE keeps darting around as we walk to my car.

"I have class after lunch, so I can't go anywhere with you," she states as we pass the picnic bench that she sat on with Lucas.

I haven't seen him at school today and wonder if she warned him. My hands ball into fists in my jacket pockets, and I remove them. The action has Layla looking up at me. The red shirt she wears hugs her small waist. Red is the best color on her. I don't reply as I click the car open.

She doesn't look happy as she climbs in. "I have your jacket in my car."

I close the door and love how close we are. I turn to Layla, gripping the steering wheel with one hand. She fidgets with her hands in her lap. "You can keep it."

Her lips appear swollen, and I love when she bites on the lower one. She shakes her head and faces the window, her profile toward me. Her swanlike neck would fit in one of my hands. I can imagine bending it to my will, bending her, fucking her. My fingers twitch like a pencil might materialize between them. I want to draw her right now.

"Evelyn and Carl want to meet you." She continues facing the window.

Her blouse gaps slightly from the side, and I can see the top swell of her breast. How the fuck does her skin look so good?

I still have the top she left in the trunk of my car. She isn't getting it back. It now resides in my bedside table.

"Do they?" I ask offhandedly.

She frowns as she faces me. "You want to meet them?" It's half a question, half a statement.

"So you told them about me?"

Her chest rises. I've hit a nerve with Layla. "They know everything about you."

I sneer. "I fucking doubt that."

Her frown deepens. "I spoke about you. You know, when Evelyn first found me." She picks at her nails as she speaks. "I mean…" Her face scrunches up. "You were gone, and I never knew…" Her eyes water, and all I want to do is drag her into my arms and hold her against my chest until the air stops filtering into her lungs.

"Never knew what?"

Her gaze dances around the car before landing back on me. "What happened to you."

"How would you, Layla?" I shift so I'm closer to her. She doesn't move. "You left and never returned." My mouth dries up as memories from that day start to seep into my system. It takes away any warmth and leaves bitterness behind.

"How could I come back?" Her breathing grows heavy. "I barely made it out alive."

The silence grows restless and I give in. "What time shall I come by your house?"

"You're not." She nods several times like she's made a decision. "I can't be around you when you're like this. I've tried. But…" She shakes her head several times. "I just can't."

Laughter licks my lips. "Well, I'm sorry to bust your fucking bubble, but you will be around me."

"Jared… Jay…" she tries, but I cut off the pleading in her voice as I move closer. "What are you doing?" Her gaze flickers to my lips.

"You want me to kiss you?" I tease.

She huffs, but I see the want in her eyes. "No," she lies.

I want a kiss, but I'm looking at my Layla, and when I'm this close to her, it's hard to believe that she's deceiving me. I reach out and she flinches. "I'd never hurt you."

She swallows. "I know, Jared." She deliberately drags out my name.

I nod. "What time should I come by your house?" I ask, softer this time.

"I'll find out what day suits them." She doesn't sound so sure.

"Don't keep me waiting."

"I'll send you the address." She tries to reach for her phone but stops when I touch her cheek, which is hot under my fingertips.

"I already know where you live. Let's get a coffee."

"I'm not leaving the school grounds."

"Neither am I." I grin and lean away from her, hating the loss immediately. I get out of the car, and Layla follows as we make our way back to the school.

"How do you know where I live?" she asks.

I spot the girl who she called Ashley lingering along the wall. She gawks at us, but Layla seems oblivious to everyone, even me. Her head is down as she walks, and I want to reach out and take her hand. She should walk with her head held high. She's worth a thousand Ashleys. I bury my hands in my jacket pockets as we walk toward the school. I open the door and let Layla go in first. "I know lots of things."

She doesn't step through immediately. "Like my phone number."

I grin. "Like your phone number."

She huffs and steps inside the school. Her nose scrunches up, and I want to kiss it, but everyone is fucking watching us—until they meet my eye and look away. Alex isn't here today, and it's working to my advantage. I can walk freely with Layla without any consequences for one day.

Layla waits outside the cafeteria. I have to issue a warning to her not to leave. When I return with two coffees, she's still standing where I left her.

I hand her a coffee, and she takes it with a ghost of a smile on her lips. We walk and it's not aimless. I'm leading her toward the library, where we won't have everyone watching us. Once again, I notice how oblivious she is to all the stares and hushed voices. She sips the coffee while peeking up at me like I might not notice.

It's cute.

I open the library door, and she steps inside. I have to stop right behind her as she pauses. As I dip my head, I inhale the scent of her hair. "What's wrong?" I whisper into her ear. Her head tilts toward my voice.

"The library?"

"It's nice and quiet." I step around her and start to walk toward the back. She's looking around her as we walk. This time she's aware of her surroundings, but luckily, only a handful of students are here. The deeper we go, the slower her footfalls become.

I spin and walk slowly backward. "I'm not going to murder you." I open my arms as far as the bookshelves on either side of me will allow.

Her mouth twitches before forming a smile that stalls my steps, and I'm moving back toward her, allowing my fingers to trail along the spine of the books. "I mean, in a library. It's too cliché."

She nods before taking a sip of her coffee. "A lake would be more appropriate." She slips under my arm, and I'm following her with a stupid fucking grin on my face.

"I wouldn't have let you drown," I counteract.

She fires a glare across her shoulder.

"I like when you're mad. I've never seen this side of you." I'm tempted to reach her and spin her around.

She tucks her hair behind her ear and sips from her coffee.

"Tell me about Evelyn and Carl."

We walk past more bookshelves as we near the back of the room.

"They're amazing." Her smile cracks the last of my anger. "I have a curfew." She's still beaming. "They're delighted when I break it." A soft laugh tumbles from her mouth. "They just want me to be happy, Jared." She stops walking and faces me. She picks idly at the lid of her coffee. "I want them to be happy too."

"Why wouldn't they be happy?" I place my cup on the edge of one of the shelves. A row of tax books is there to rest my hand against.

"They love me."

I love you.

"I can't have them upset," she finishes.

I push away from the shelf and step closer. The bookshelves don't allow her to go anywhere. "You think I'd upset them?"

Her mouth moves, but no words come out as my gaze glides to her lips. "Yes," she whispers.

"Why's that?" I touch her neck, and her eyes flutter closed at the contact.

"Jared." My name sounds like a plea.

I put pressure on her neck, and her eyes snap open. "Why's that?" I repeat.

She shuffles back, but there's nowhere to go. "They're very protective."

My gut twists. I let my fingers trail down her neck. "I'm very protective too. Or have you forgotten?" I whisper into her ear.

"I'd never forget you." Her voice shakes.

My cock hardens. Words I've always wanted to hear just spilled from her mouth. A mouth I capture with my own. Her warm, moist lips have my control slipping further, and when Layla kisses me back, every ounce of hate or anger I've been holding on to vanishes, and all I want is her. All I truly want is her.

I tilt her head so I have more access to her pretty lips. My tongue sinks into her mouth, and I taste coffee and lust on her tongue. I push my body against her, and she groans. Her face fills both my hands as I grip her, wanting to control each movement so I have complete access to her mouth. I want to savor every single second with Layla.

"Jared." Her voice is breathless as I give her lips a break and kiss her jawline.

"When I fuck you, it's going to be painfully slow."

Her hands reach up and grip my arms as I continue to hold her face. Her pulse pounds along her neck, and I press a kiss to her frantic heartbeat.

"I've waited too long." I look her in the eyes. "I want to explore every part of you. My mouth will touch every single inch of your skin."

She inhales sharply, and if I don't step away now, I'm not going to be able to stop myself.

I don't step away. "I want to taste you, Layla."

Her eyes widen, yet she doesn't run. She's staring up at me, and I've never wanted to defile someone so much. "Would you like that?"

"Ms. Masters, Mr. McGivney. Fornicating in the library is against school policy."

The brightness seeps from Layla's eyes, and fear takes over.

I'm spinning, blocking her from Coach. I want to plow his fucking face in for frightening her.

I grin and nod. "Teachers fucking students is definitely against school policy, too."

His face reddens with a temper as he steps toward me. "How dare you."

I meet his steps. "Lucy—is that your latest victim? You sound like a right pedophile to me."

His mouth opens, and a vein bulges along his neck.

"Is that why you're creeping around the library? Watching young girls? Your wife would be appalled."

He grits his teeth, but I know when I have someone by the balls. "Maybe I should tell her."

"Jared." Layla's voice is low, but I curse her internally for calling me by that name.

Coach doesn't even seem to notice; he appears ready to throw up. He just better not fucking do it near me. "Now listen, you fucking donkey. You breathe one word, and I'll let everyone know what a creep you are."

He doesn't say anything but scrambles away.

"Jesus, Jared."

I reach back for Layla's hand to give her comfort as I make sure Coach is gone, but her fingers are yanked from my hand, making me face her.

"You can't..." She shakes her head. "You can't talk to a teacher like that." She frowns. "Or me." Her words are an afterthought. "I'm going to be late."

She's ready to dart past me, but I stop her. My hand circles her wrist. "Monday, we're having lunch together again." My gut tightens.

Layla doesn't rush off. "Fine, I'll be there."

"Okay." I release her, not happy that a whole weekend separates us.

She's still staring up at me.

"Go before you're late."

She nods and quickly leaves. I watch her until she disappears around the bookshelves and out of sight. It causes such instant emptiness that it shocks me into moving.

Like I could even run away from the void.

CHAPTER SEVENTEEN

LAYLA

I'M IN A DAZE as I leave the library. Everything in me burns. The cold air outside doesn't do much to cool me down. I should be in class, but after that kiss... My tongue flicks out, and I lick my lips. As I make my way to my car, I tug my bag up on my shoulder. I need to text Jared and tell him he can't meet Evelyn or Carl. I can't do this. I need time to think. His words about kissing every inch of my skin have me walking faster. I hate how badly I want him.

I get into my car and don't look around as I leave the parking lot. I blare a classical music station to get my mind off Jared, but forgetting him is like forgetting to breathe. My mind would burn as violently as my lungs would, and it would fill with Jared just as my lungs would fill themselves with air.

My breath grows frantic, and I have no idea what's happening to me. My vision dims, and I pull in off the road.

"Let it out." I speak out loud to give myself permission to cry. No tears come, and my laughter is angry and bitter. I lean against the headrest and take in my surroundings. A small grocery store is what I've pulled up outside of. I didn't eat lunch with Jared. I'm not hungry, but I know I should eat something. Since my body wouldn't allow me to cry, I grip my bag and make my way into the grocery store.

The overhead music is soft, and the air conditioner is on full blast. My light blouse doesn't take the bite out of the air that brushes my skin, but I welcome the cold as it steals some of the heat.

I'm roaming aimlessly down the aisle when someone walks toward me a little too closely. I look up, and the moment I see Kieran, he smiles. He steps into my personal space and gives me one of those half hugs with one arm. It's seriously awkward on my part. He doesn't seem to notice.

His blond hair is pushed back out of his face. The Aran beige sweater looks way too heavy for the warm weather we're having today. Along with dark brown trousers and heavy boots, he looks ready for a fishing boat.

"Fancy meeting you here." He speaks with laughter, his eyes baby blue and bright. I feel like I'm caught up in a whirlwind, or maybe it's like I've just walked out of one. A tornado would be more fitting.

"Yeah."

He nudges my arm. "Still the talker, I see."

I smile at his stupid words and grin. "Yeah, a real chatter-box."

Surprise lights up his face, and he laughs. "So, how have you been? Any more parties?" He folds his arms and dips his head, waiting for my answer. I would have stuffed my hands into my pockets if I had any. Instead, I let them hang on either side of me so I'm aware of them. I shrug. "Yeah, great. Just school, no more parties. I'm actually babysitting tonight." *God, why did I tell him that?* He's a stranger, after all.

He nods. "Let me check my calendar." Kieran pauses while staring briefly at the ceiling, confusing me until he looks back at me with a smile. "Nope, it's all clear. I can babysit with you."

Heat blazes across my face. "Kieran, I'm not trying to be rude, but I wasn't inviting you."

He clutches his chest. "What a way to shoot a guy down."

I'm shaking my head like a crazy person. "No, no. It's just I can't invite you to someone else's house." Mortification is burning a permanent red mark into my skin.

"So you would go on a date with me?"

This conversation has taken a nosedive. Now I'm stuttering. "Hmm... I... I..."

"It's cool. Maybe another time," Kieran says, not looking at all fazed by my response.

I nod my head, and he nudges my arm again.

"Great seeing you, Layla." He steps around me and moves toward the fridge.

"Yeah, you too, Kieran."

What a strange day. I leave the shop, not buying anything, and climb into my car. I start the engine right away. Before backing up and leaving, I glance in my rearview mirror to make sure no cars are coming.

My phone rings, and I put it on speakerphone without looking at the caller ID.

"Hello."

"Hi, sweetheart. Just calling to let you know I won't be home. I got called into the hospital, and Carl has to work late again." Evelyn's words have me sinking back into the seat.

"I'm actually babysitting for someone," I say, hoping she doesn't ask where. Ashley sent me her address, and the area doesn't have the best rep. I don't want to worry Evelyn.

"Oh. For who?" Her voice raises a few bars. I have a social life all of a sudden. It surprises me too.

"Ashley, a friend from school." I flip the turn signal to make a left onto the road.

Evelyn seems happy that I'm getting out more and ends the conversation with "Okay, well, I'm headed out the door. But I'll call you later."

I say my goodbyes and hang up.

***

When I get home, Evelyn is gone. There's a buzz in my head while I shower. So much stuff flows around, and it's hard to concentrate on just one thing. I keep wanting to check my phone, keep waiting for Jared to text. I miss him. I think I'm starting to become immune to the chaos he causes to my emotions.

What is wrong with me?

I spend the time grabbing food and flicking through the TV channels before I have to leave for Ashley's.

The area in which Ashley lives is one you wouldn't walk through at night. I've never been there, but I have heard about it. But people can be vicious with words, and rumors are rumors for a reason. Yeah, maybe it isn't as bad as I think.

My black leggings still have that soft, fluffy feeling that I know will soon be gone. But right now, they make me feel warm and cozy. Throwing on an oversized army green sweater and slipping into my white tennis shoes, I run my fingers through my hair. I'm kind of lucky like that; my fingers are as effective as a brush.

On the way to Ashley's, my mind runs rampant with awful scenarios. The tang of blood makes me stop chewing my lip. Scenarios like being held at gunpoint to being beaten by some drug addict. I take a left; two large arched red brick walls sit on either side of me as I pass through the large black gates.

The entrance is very grand, but that's where the curb appeal stops. Rows and rows of trailers line the large site. Small patches of grass cut off by small fences or random items cut up the yard space. An old brown sofa with one missing cushion sits on the sidewalk. The grime and holes tell the story of its abandonment. I pull up to the trailer that has "7" on a small wooden sign out front. Turning off the car, I get out my phone and ring Ashley. Drumming my fingers on the steering wheel, I watch the trailer for any sign of movement as I wait for Ashley to answer. The phone rings out and goes straight to voicemail.

She said number seven. I could just take a chance and knock on the door. It's nearly dark, and no lamps light up the site, only small pockets of light from some of the other trailers' windows, just not Ashley's.

I squeal when my phone rings, and a shaky laugh leaves my mouth as I look at the caller ID.

"Hi, Ashley. I'm not sure if I'm in the right place, but I'm parked at the front of site number seven," I say while my heart calms down.

"Give me one second." I can hear the coos of a baby. "Oh, I see you."

The phone clicks off, and the door opens, letting light pour out. Ashley waves at me as she stands on the step with Nicco on her hip. Jumping out of the car, I throw my phone in my bag and lock the car doors as I head up to meet Ashley on the step. Ashley has the door open and wears a warm smile as she lets me in.

"You are a godsend," she tells me, but my attention is on Nicco.

Cute isn't the word. He's even more adorable in person than in his photos. Little hands reach out for me, and I look at Ashley first for permission. She hands over Nicco, and I wait for him to cry, but he doesn't. His large brown eyes examine my face while his chubby little fingers touch everything his eyes take in.

"You guys are bonding well. So, I'm going to get ready." Ashley smiles at me and closes the front door.

"No problem. Nicco and I will just hang out here." I speak in baby talk.

Ashley laughs. "You're a natural," she says while leaving the room.

I love children. They just carry such innocence and honesty that most adults don't. They are simple, and once you feed them and play with them, all's right with the world.

As Nicco plays with my hair, making cooing noises, I sit down on the sizable beige sofa that rests under the window. All the curtains are open, making me feel exposed. The trailer is a lot larger than I previously thought. This room serves as a kitchen and den area, with everything that a regular house would have. An arch leads into a hallway that Ashley went down. The TV now catches Nicco's attention, so I turn it up. A large bear roams through a real forest and Nicco laughs. His little white onesie leaves his chubby legs bare. I turn up the TV so we can hear what the bear is saying.

When Ashley comes back out, I'm shocked. "Wow, you look stunning."

She smiles, showcasing her snow-white teeth. With a killer skin-tight white dress and red heels, she looks ready for the catwalk. She's beautiful every day at college, but tonight, she'll turn a lot of heads. She doesn't look like a woman who's had a baby.

I get the rundown of what Nicco needs: just one more bottle before bed, which will be in twenty minutes. There's Coke and chocolate in the fridge, and she shows me where Nicco's bedroom is, along with the bathroom. The trailer is nice; it's clear Ashley really takes pride in her home.

"I'm nervous. I've only ever left him once."

I can understand that. "Go and enjoy yourself. If anything happens, I promise I'll call you," I say.

She gives Nicco several kisses before getting her bag and coat. "Seriously, Layla, you are a godsend," she tells me before leaving. I lock the door and wait until I feel she's out of sight before closing all the curtains.

"That's better, isn't it?" I ask Nicco, and he smiles.

Nicco goes down with no problem, and I get myself a Coke from the fridge. It's only nine thirty, and I don't expect Ashley back anytime soon, so the knock on the trailer door sends my heart skyrocketing.

I sit still, clutching the remote, listening. But it's all gone silent. Whoever it was has left. The knock on the glass behind me has me jumping up. I clamp my hand over my mouth to contain the squeal that wants to emerge. I don't want to wake Nicco. But the person outside is now back at the front door calling Ashley's name, and he isn't going away. That gives me a little relief, knowing it isn't a burglar or anything. I answer the door.

I nearly fall back as Chester pushes his way in. He's down the hall before I can even get my bearings together.

He bursts back into the room. "Where is she?"

His anger and hostility have me frozen. I'm shaking my head, trying to say she isn't here, but the words get lodged in my throat.

"I know you can speak. Your mouth sure moves fast when you're talking to Jay." He licks his lips with a sneer on his face, but his tone is still angry, hostile.

He isn't violent like you, I want to say. But as he takes a step toward me, I back up, not able to say a word.

"Listen, bitch, tell me where she is." His raised voice ricochets around the space, which feels tiny now. Nicco's cry unfreezes me, and I dart around Chester, only to have him pull me back. His touch ignites an old fear. It's like Bert is looking down at me, and I can feel my lip tremble as my body locks up. I'm looking at him, but I can't see properly. The insistent cry of Nicco once again has me moving, and I pull my arm out of Chester's hold.

"Nicco's crying," I say with a heavy tongue. I have trouble forcing the words out. My speaking seems to make Chester realize how threatening he is, and he takes a step back and lets me get to Nicco. My breaths become raspy as I rock Nicco, and the tremble in my hands grows worse. The need to cry is choking me.

What am I going to do? First, I need to calm down.

My breathing settles, and soon Nicco is asleep on my chest. I put him back in the crib, and I want nothing more than to stay there and hide until Ashley comes home. Maybe five or ten minutes have passed, but it feels like forever. Chester is silent in the den. I can only wish that means he's left. With Bert, me staying silent or hiding got me the worst beatings. It was always easier to face him. But I never could. Looking down at Nicco, I swallow the tears of self-pity. I don't want to bring Chester in here, on top of an innocent child. Jared spent his whole life protecting me. To step out of this room will be huge for me, but I will for the baby.

I'm not like Jared; my steps are unsure and clumsy. Trying to push my fear away, I tell myself this isn't Bert. This is just a boy with anger issues who is looking for a girl. My heart jumps when the couch comes into view. Chester sits on it, his elbows resting on his knees while he stares at me.

"Now tell me where she is." His words are calm and low, but they still hold a threat.

Sweat makes the base of my neck itchy, but I don't dare scratch the skin. I move as slowly as possible. It's an old trick, one that seemed to infuriate Bert, like it's annoying Chester right now.

"Fuck's sake. I swear, I don't know what the fuck Jay sees in you." He stands, and I stop moving.

Layla, speak, and this will end, I tell myself. But words once again fail me, and dread curls its cruel hands around my throat.

CHAPTER EIGHTEEN

LAYLA

U SE YOUR WORDS.

"She went out and asked me to mind Nicco." There. That wasn't so hard. I would have been pleased with myself, but Chester doesn't seem happy with my answer.

"I can see she's not here. Out where?" His clenched fists have me taking a step back. My back hits the wall. "I don't know," I answer honestly and praise myself once again for speaking.

"Dumbass white bitch."

I pick a spot on the floor as he walks to the fridge, helping himself to a drink. Tears burn my eyes. Tears that I refuse to let fall.

"You really are stupid."

I glance up at Chester as he gulps down the full Coke before burping loudly. My hands shake as I roll them into fists. Heat travels up my neck until it scorches my cheeks. "I think you should leave." God, I wish my voice sounded stronger. It's as weak as a newborn kitten.

He laughs at me before taking a step closer. "Don't think. Just get on the phone and call Ashley."

I don't hesitate. I want out of this situation. I can't even stay unscratched for a day. The old fear is there in full force like I'm ten again.

I keep one eye on Chester as he walks around the trailer. Ashley answers. Loud music pumps behind her.

"Ashley, this is Layla. Chester's here," I say.

"What?" She sounds like she's moving; the background noise becomes more distant. The phone is swiped from my hand as Chester starts to shout down the phone.

"Where the fuck are you? Whoring around?" He sneers. "No, I won't. He's my son."

Chester is Nicco's dad? Oh, the poor kid.

I move away from him and find myself at the door. My bag sits on the sideboard with my keys in it.

"You left our son with this stupid bitch."

I freeze once again at the hateful words.

"I'll call her what I want. Get home, now." He throws my phone at me. I don't catch it; instead, it hits the ground and separates into three parts. "You can leave."

My heart rate seems to slow, and my feet feel like lead. "No." I want nothing more than to leave, but what if he gets mad and hurts Nicco? I would never forgive myself.

He snorts before sitting back on the couch and flicking through the TV stations. Meanwhile, I stand rigidly at the door, just listening for Ashley. The beat of my heart is all I can hear. I try to calm myself and stop the onslaught of thoughts. I focus on picking up my phone and putting it back together as quietly as possible. But Chester glances at me every few moments.

My phone isn't broken and switches on straight away. Six missed calls from Ashley. I don't call her back for fear of provoking Chester. It doesn't take much to set him off. The silence in the room makes me aware that the TV has been silenced. I glance up slowly, and Chester stares back at me. The anger he displayed earlier is gone.

"So how do you know Jay?"

Really? He wants to chat after all that? But if he's calm until Ashley gets here, that's all that matters.

"We grew up together," I manage to say, with only a slight tremor in my voice.

He sits back, scratching his face with the remote, which I will never touch again. "Yeah, he mentioned that, but not much more."

He's waiting for me to expand on the matter, but I'm not going to. I don't want to tell him anything about me, most certainly not about my past. The fact that Jared even mentioned me to Chester makes me think they were close in some way. I want to answer just to keep things flowing, but my tongue grows heavy in my mouth, so I just nod.

He snorts and sits back, flicking through the stations but not turning up the volume.

"Jared's doing well here, you know." The look he gives me causes a shiver to chase up the back of my legs. He waves his hand in my direction. "We don't need white girls comin' in, stirring up shit."

I swallow the lump that's forming in my throat as I glance at the distorted glass on the front door. I'm just waiting for the light of a car to reflect off it, or a shadow to appear.

Come on, Ashley.

I back further into the wall as Chester gets up, yanking up his jeans as he walks toward me.

"Why you actin' like a little mouse?"

I almost can't hear his words over the roar of blood in my ears.

This isn't happening.

Chester is in front of me, one arm leaning against the wall only a few inches from my head. "I don't like you." His eyes roam my face, and I hold my breath until black spots appear in front of my eyes. The noise of keys in the door has me almost falling to the ground in relief. Ashley bursts in, along with the smell of alcohol and perfume.

"What are you..." Her glance jumps from Chester to me. "Are you okay?" Her hand goes to her hip as her head swings back to Chester. "Did you touch her?"

I blink as all the sound comes rushing back to me.

Chester looks me up and down like I am nothing, and the tips of my ears burn.

Tutting, he doesn't answer Ashley.

I move, grabbing my bag off the counter. "I'll leave you to it." I can't bear being in the room with him for one more moment. I'm out the door, not stopping as Ashley follows me. The night carries with it a soft spray of rain. The type that soaks you without you knowing.

"Layla, wait."

I don't stop but get my keys out of my bag. It gives Ashley the chance to catch up with me.

"What did he do?" It's the fear in her voice that makes me pause. Turning to her, I have so much I want to say. Like how did she, for one second, allow him near her? She seems so nice and put together.

"He didn't touch me, if that's what you're asking," I tell her. Her white dress is getting wet now, making it partially see-through. "Will you be okay with him?" I have to ask because as much as I want to run, looking at Ashley in her see-through dress, I'm not thrilled with the idea of her being alone with him.

"I can handle Chester." She takes a deep breath. "I'm sorry about this," she says.

"I'd better go." I open the car door and jump in, yet I don't leave until Ashley is back in her trailer.

The whole drive home, I tell myself it's okay to cry, but no tears come.

***

I wake to my alarm ringing and a headache. Flailing my hand toward the screeching device, hoping to hit it and turn the bloody thing off, doesn't help; the alarm clock continues to ring. That's when I realize the sound isn't coming from my alarm, but my phone. Wiping the sleep out of my eyes, I answer it.

"You're a hard woman to track down."

I sit up straight in the bed, wide awake. "Jared. Hi."

My stomach quivers.

"I texted you last night, and when I got no reply, I started to worry."

"Sorry, I had an early night." I take the phone away from my face to see I have several messages.

"Yeah, I was chatting with Kieran, and he told me you were babysitting for Ashley."

I freeze at that, the whole night slowly trickling back in like a broken tap.

"You there?" Jared asks, and I try to shake off the night before.

"Yeah, sorry. I didn't know you knew Kieran."

"I didn't know you did."

That's fair enough. But I don't want to get into this conversation. "So... is everything okay?" I ask, pushing off the duvet.

"There's a party tonight. Do you want to go?" Jared sounds unsure. I don't understand why.

"I'm not really into parties," I say, getting out of bed and pulling back the curtains. The sun beams in through the window, and I pull them closed. I need to get some painkillers.

"It's not really a request."

"Then why ask?" I need the painkillers a little more now that I've been standing.

"I'm trying to be polite."

"If I say no?"

"What do you think?"

Is that anger I hear in his voice?

"Great. I have to go, Jared." I hang up and go downstairs. I check out the house to discover I'm home alone. That often happens if Evelyn gets called into the hospital late. She'll stay the night with the child who'd been brought in.

She'd done that with me when I was taken to the hospital. I didn't speak to her then. I can still remember when she walked into the room.

I haven't spoken one word in nine days. I've had so many people arrive and try to make me open up, only to realize I'm not talking. They always leave, but today is different.

A woman with soft brown eyes enters. She doesn't acknowledge me but merely sits down on a chair, takes out a magazine, and starts reading. I lie patiently for fifteen minutes as she flicks through her glossy magazine. Finally, she looks at me with a smile. When I glance away, she starts rummaging in her bag. Curiosity gets the better of me, and I watch as she takes out a pack of Oreos. She stuffs one into her mouth and then eats two more before offering me one. I don't know why, but I take it. As I pray she'll offer me another one, she eats the rest of the pack and crumbles up the package. I feel disappointed. To my surprise, she gets up and stuffs the magazine into her bag and leaves my room. I'm floored. I reach for the buzzer, tempted to call the nurse and tell her that someone just hung out in my room, read a magazine, ate all the Oreos, and left. The door opens and a nurse comes in. I drop the buzzer and remain quiet as they change my drip and refill my water. Instead, I stare at the ceiling, wondering where Jared is and what will happen to us.

The next day, the same woman who ate the Oreos arrives to my room with a breakfast roll that makes my mouth water. The hospital food is bland, and I push each meal away. She starts to eat it. I'm not sure what is going on. Then she pauses and takes a second roll wrapped in foil from her backpack and hands it to me. I take the roll, and as I munch on it, I discover food is my weakness. When my belly is full of real food, I lie back.

"Thank you." My voice sounds strange after not using it for such a long time.

"You're welcome. I'm Evelyn."

She reaches out her hand, and I take it. "Layla."

She smiles, the corners of her eyes crinkling.

"I'm a counselor." That surprises me. I wasn't sure what she was going to say, but she doesn't look like a counselor. All the rest of them have been persistent and just snotty. Like they feel like they have to fix something because it's broken and check it off their lists.

With Evelyn, there's a kindness that makes me want to talk to her and tell her everything I've suffered.

"Is there anything I can do for you?" Evelyn tidies up the papers from our rolls as she speaks.

"Yes, there is."

She stops what she's doing and turns to me. Her face looks serious as she waits.

"Jared... Jared was in the house with me. I want to know if he's safe."

She nods. "Do you know his last name?"

I look away. "No. None of us do. It's just Jared."

She pauses, and I wonder if she's going to say no. "Okay. I'll try to find out." Her words give me hope and have me sitting up a bit straighter.

"When?" I don't want to be pushy, but I need to know he's safe.

"I'll go now." She speaks with a softness that matches her kind smile.

"Thank you, Evelyn."

Her smile widens. "You're welcome, Layla."

I get the bottle of aspirin out of the medicine cabinet and take two with a large glass of water before going back to bed. But of course, I can't sleep.

Bzzz. Another text message.

I'm sorry about last night.

It's from Ashley. I chew on my lip, thinking about what to write back. It isn't her fault Chester showed up, but I still hate that she didn't tell me he's Nicco's father. Would I have babysat if I had known?

I groan before texting her back.

It's cool. It's not your fault. Hope you and Nicco are okay.

I look at the other messages; all three are from Jared.

Where are you?

Answer me now.

You're babysitting? You should have told me. At least I know you're safe.

Safe. I was the furthest thing from safe last night.

I lie in bed for a while. My mind keeps wandering to Jared. No matter how much I try to pull my thoughts away from him, I can't. He's safe. I smile, really letting that fact sink in. He isn't just safe; he's in my life. He has a father and friends. The smile slips when I think of Alex. Will she be there tonight? Jared said she isn't his girlfriend, but I wonder if she knows that.

Should I go? I grab my phone off my nightstand and open up the last message from Jared, staring at it longer than is normal. I close the phone before flopping back on the bed.

"Everything alright?"

I bounce back up as quickly as I had flopped down. "I didn't know you were home." I clutch my heart as Carl opens my curtains with amusement on his face.

"Came home last night. I found a note from Evelyn saying you were babysitting." Carl faces me now.

"Yeah, for a girl from school." I sound calm; I'm not on the inside—my heart pounds.

"Did you have fun?" he asks, stepping away from me.

"Oh yeah, loads," I say.

He smiles again as I turn to face him. He stands at the door, one hand on the frame.

"Who called you this morning?"

Heat scorches my cheeks. He was listening. I go over the conversation in my head. Nothing bad was said, so why the hell am I burning up?

"It was Jared. He was inviting me to a party."

Carl seems stiff; his hand tightens on the door. "That was nice of him." I can hear the forced calm that he puts into his voice.

"Yeah, it was." I start to make my bed just to give myself something to do and hope that it ends this conversation. As I move around to the opposite side, I notice Carl is still watching me and has some internal battle going on behind his eyes.

"You should go."

I still at his words, then slowly turn toward him. "You think?" I ask, narrowing my eyes slightly, wondering where he's going with this.

He gives a quick laugh. "Yes, I do. And don't look so suspicious. You deserve it."

My cheeks heat, and I nod. "Thanks, Carl," I say. His words mean so much to me. He nods back before gently tapping the door and leaving.

I get dressed in my gardening clothes. It's something I love to do. My army green long-sleeved top fits me snugly, and I drag my overalls over my legs before getting into my old, tattered tennis shoes.

After piling my hair on top of my head, I grab a granola bar, my knee pads, and the key to the shed.

A gentle breeze caresses my skin as I step outside into the heat. It's going to be a hot day. For February in Ireland, that's unusual, so I intend to soak up the pleasant weather. I eat the granola bar as I drop my knee pads beside the line of shrubs I've been working on. Carl and Evelyn are so great at letting me dig up and plant their yard. They told me that it saved them from hiring a landscaper. Their compliment meant a lot to me.

I think back to when I first started gardening. I wasn't good at anything, really, or at least I didn't think so. One day, I decided to tackle the overgrown and unloved yard, and they seemed genuinely amazed at how much I had done. It was my way of giving something back to them.

After removing rocks and mowing the lawn, I had a far better idea of what area I had to work with. I spent a few days drawing out a plan of what I was going to do. Carl and Evelyn said I should plant some shrubs along the paved path that curved through the yard. I had never planted a flower in my life, so that had been a first. The idea of giving life to something made me excited.

I know that sounds silly, but I spent so much of my life watching things being caged and suppressed, that watching plants grow and blossom gave me hope.

The yard is square; there's a large brick wall six feet high in the rear with wooden fencing on either side, and it's clean and easy to work on.

Carl had to help me create the concrete circle I wanted. In the middle of the yard, he cut out a circle of sod, and he poured the circle for me. He did a great job. Him being an engineer helped with the measurements. Along the left side of the developing garden, we framed up flower beds with railroad ties that we repurposed from the local train tracks that were being rebuilt. Once stained and set, they looked great. I painted the back wall white and stained the fence with the same brown as the ties. Now I'm starting to plant.

I grab my gloves and trowel and pick up the lavender plants that I'm going to place in the center of the concrete area. The smell of the small green plants is intoxicating, and I inhale the scent. They're still young, but when they grow, they will bloom with lavender-colored flowers. The images on the plant markers that came with them look great.

How many people my age find peace in gardening? Morgan's idea of peace is shopping or going to parties. To me, that's torture. My back is to the sliding door as I plant; the swish sound of it opening has me sitting back on my heels while wiping off the sweat that's gathered on my forehead. Wearing heavy overalls in the heat we're experiencing is crazy, but I feel comfortable, and they are my gardening clothes. I shield my eyes as I turn to Carl. I hope he likes what I've done.

I look in the general direction of the door and blink, not sure if what I'm seeing is a mirage. Brown eyes, banked by broad cheekbones and a mouth that is partially open, watch me.

Jared.

CHAPTER NINETEEN

JARED 24 HOURS BEFORE

I LEAVE THE LIBRARY with a raging hard-on. My mind jumps to Alex. She would blow me if I found her. My cock starts to die instantly at the thought of anyone other than Layla touching me. I've entered the main hall when my attention is snagged on Layla as she races out the front door of the college.

"Hi, Jay," some guy, who I think is Jack, calls across the hall. I ignore him and all the other greetings.

Layla said she was going to class. My feet tear up the floor as I follow her. My phone rings as I burst out of the front doors. She's speed walking to her car as I answer the phone without looking at the caller ID. I don't dare take my gaze off Layla as she gets into her car.

"Jay, how are you?"

Rex's voice steals my focus. "Is everything okay?" I ask. Rex isn't someone who rings randomly, and the thoughts of anything happening to him has me covering my other ear so I'm blocking out all sounds around me.

"Yeah, I just need to swap your training around. Could you come in tomorrow instead of today?"

I look back up as Layla drives out the school gates.

Fuck.

I start walking to my car. "Yeah, that's no problem, Rex."

"Good man. I have a new member I couldn't say no to."

I get into the car and turn on the ignition. "Who?" I ask.

"Warren O'Reagan."

That makes me pause. "I know him."

Rex is silent, and I can just imagine what he's thinking. "Jay, he isn't someone you should be around."

"He goes to my college, and I actually like him. But I don't get involved in his family life."

Rex snorts. "That's why I couldn't turn him down. I don't want to make an enemy of the O'Reagans."

"They're good to have on your side."

I grin as Rex snorts again. "Time will tell."

"Speaking of time, is three good tomorrow?"

"Sure. I'll see you then."

I hang up and leave the school grounds. Layla is long gone, and I have no idea which way she went. Ringing her phone is futile. I drive straight and get lucky as I see her pulling out of a grocery store. What makes me pull in is the guy who's standing outside with his hand still raised in the air as he stares after Layla's car.

My blood roars in my veins, and I pull up, ripping up gravel and missing Kieran by millimeters. He's the guy from Chester's house, the one who inquired about Layla. I roll down the window and smile like I didn't just nearly run him over.

"What's up, Kieran?"

"Apart from you nearly killing me, I'm good." He shifts his grocery bag into his other hand.

"Sorry, I didn't see you."

Like fuck you didn't see me shines in Kieran's eyes, but he's wise enough not to voice it. Chester must have educated him about who I am after I left the party the other night.

I look in the direction Layla's car disappeared down and now regret my decision to stop. "You know Layla?" I ask.

Kieran smiles, and I want to wipe the look off his face. "Yeah, she's cool. A little quiet, but pretty cool."

I force a smile. "Yeah, I was trying to get in touch with her."

"I don't have her number, but she's babysitting tonight. That's all she told me."

Babysitting?

"For who?"

Kieran laughs. "What are you, the Gardaí?"

I don't react.

Kieran's smile melts off his face. "She didn't say who."

I rev the car and nearly crush his toes as I tear after Layla, but I have no idea where she went.

Where are you? I send the text as I drive aimlessly. I'm tempted to go back and kill Kieran. I need a release, and Rex canceling my session today really hits home.

I continue to drive and fire another text to Layla.

Answer me.

Ringing her again doesn't get me answers. Does she really think she can ignore me? I drive to her house, and some part of me relaxes when I see her car in her driveway. I'm still pissed she's ignoring me.

I check the time. My father is returning home from London, and he wants a word. I have a fair idea it will be about Layla. She isn't going anywhere for now. I take one final look at her house before I drive home.

***

"Welcome home, Master Jay." William is waiting for me in the hallway. I've never given much thought to him, but I pause.

"Do you live here?"

"Pardon, Master Jay?"

"Do you have a family, William?"

He seems flustered but answers me. "Yes, Master Jay. I have two daughters and a son. They are grown up now."

"Do you see them much?"

William appears even more uncomfortable. "Sometimes, Master Jay."

I nod, realizing I'm fucking useless at small talk and have no idea why I care about William all of a sudden. "Is my father here?"

William's features settle with contentment now that we're no longer discussing him. "He's in his study waiting for you, Master Jay."

I check my phone to see if Layla has returned my calls or messages, but she hasn't. Placing my phone on silent, I enter the study. My father is on a ladder pulling a book from a top shelf. I could knock the ladder over. I'm sure the fall would snap his neck. I'm picturing him lying on the ground, his head at an odd angle, blood pooling around the crown of his head, seeping across the wooden floor, reflecting the bookshelves in a distorted image.

My father glances at me and starts to climb down, hugging a book like it's treasure. "You brought her into my home."

I don't have to ask who he's referring to. I know who. Our home has cameras in every corner. I never expected Layla to go undetected. "I was under the impression that this was my home too."

My father walks to his desk, not showing any emotion until he drops the book heavily on his desk. The noise bounces around the large space. My father's lips rise slightly, and it's not a smile—more of a grimace. "I remember when I found you after years of searching."

Everything in me grows rigid. My father never speaks about what happened in his life before he found me.

"Bringing you into my home." He steeples his fingers against the book cover. "Helping you become the son I lost."

"Lost." I repeat the odd word and take a step toward my father. "I was in the foster system. Something I've often wondered about."

My father stands up straight. "You never asked."

"You never spoke of it, so I assumed it was off-limits."

"Nothing in this world is off-limits to us." *Except Layla.* My father's smile is foreign to me. "Your mother put you there. I already told you that."

That still hurts like fuck, but I bury the pain quickly. "You never told me why."

He shrugs. "I don't know."

"Where is she now?" I ask. I hate her.

"I don't know."

It's my turn to sneer. "You don't know much."

My father's features grow tense before he waves a hand dismissively in the air, the large silver watch that he always wears on his wrist catching the light. "Evelyn Masters tracked you down two years ago. I warned her to stay away, but she didn't listen."

Evelyn. Layla's adoptive mother. It takes me a moment to process what my father is saying. "You knew where Layla was two years ago?" My accusatory voice drips with venom that turns my tongue heavy.

"Layla has known where you were for two years," my father reinforces. "Now she is here for your wealth."

My father's greedy fingers open the book in front of him, like he has made his point and I should leave.

"She can have every single fucking penny."

His head snaps up. His brows drag down. "What did you say?"

"You heard me. She can have it all."

"Have you lost your mind?"

"No." I grin. "You knew where she was, and you didn't tell me."

My father tuts like I'm being an errant child. "If I had informed you, you would have set off and made a fool of yourself. Since she already knew you were here, she clearly didn't care."

He's fucking lying. Layla didn't know. Layla cares. I can tell when she lies, and that day at the gym—seeing me shook her to the core.

"That was my decision to make."

"Women make men weak." My father's voice rises, and he steps away from his desk.

"This isn't about me. It's about you. Are you still bitter that Maura left you?" Saying my mother's name pierces my heart, but it drags more anger from my father.

"You will mind your tongue."

"Will I now?" I give a smug smirk, feeling giddy from standing up to him.

He stares at me before his anger settles, and he starts to think. "Very well, Jay." He walks away, plotting his next move.

"She's off-limits," I say to his back.

He doesn't respond.

"Layla is not to be touched." I continue walking to his desk and stop when he unbuttons his suit jacket and sits back down while looking up at me.

"Your mother hid you from me. Hid you in the foster system so I wouldn't find you."

His confession floors me, but I still cling to my conviction that he is not to touch Layla. "Layla is a good person," I start.

His fist hits his desk heavily. "Listen to me, boy. Everything that happened to you was inflicted by your mother's actions. And now, Layla is causing a rift between us. Look at yourself." My father rises.

I try to control the darkness that swirls inside me. My mother hid me from my father.

"Why?" The question doesn't rattle him.

"Why what?" He sits back down.

"Why did Maura hide me from you?"

My father shrugs. "I don't know."

More lies.

I can't look away from him as he pretends I don't exist. Calling him out on his lies will get me nowhere. The information he just gave me is the most I've gotten in years. "I'll be the son you need me to be," I say.

My father nods, and his shoulders relax. He's happy with my response.

"As long as Layla remains safe."

His jaw tightens as his eyes flash with fury. "If you want to be a fool for that girl, then be a fool." I'm waiting for more, but my father bends his head, picks up a pen, and starts writing in the open journal in front of him. "You can leave, Jay."

Disappointment isn't something I've heard in his voice, and I've never given it much thought, but I want to erase the tone from his mouth and never hear it again. I'm staring at the crown of his head, waiting for him to look back up, but after a few minutes, when he continues to ignore me, I leave his study.

William is outside the door when I exit my father's den. "Master Jay, Miss Alexandra is waiting for you in your quarters."

I nod at William, unable to say anything, and make my way upstairs. I haven't cleared the last step before she harasses me.

"I didn't take you for someone who was weak, Jay." Her smile stretches her ruby red lips across straight white teeth.

"I'm not in the fucking mood, Alex," I warn, and her smile dims but doesn't disappear completely.

"I can see that. Mark is having a party tomorrow night on his private beach. So I'll need you to pick me up at eight."

I pull off my jacket and throw it on the chair. William has a fire lit, and I'm drawn to the heat, or maybe it's the distance from Alex.

I thought she would start about me leaving school with Layla and how I nearly ran over her, but she doesn't say a word about it. She missed school on Friday too. I wonder what she's plotting.

"Jay, we have to be there. It's important to Mark." Alex has moved beside me.

I glance at her. "I'll be there."

She smiles victoriously. "Good."

"But you will have to find a way there yourself. I won't be picking you up." I move away from the fire.

"Why is that?"

I face Alex. "Because I'm taking someone else."

She doesn't react straight away. "I don't think I need to ask who."

"Then don't."

She moves closer. Her hand reaches out and touches the belt of my trousers. "You seem tense. Let me fix that for you."

I brush her hand away. "I'm not tense."

She exhales. "Tell me what you want. Sex?" Alex tugs at her top, and I don't stop her. The red material floats to the ground. "Let's have sex if it takes the scowl off your face." She reaches back and unclips her bra. It joins her top on the floor, releasing her artificial breasts. When she reaches for my trousers, I stop her by gripping her wrists. She looks me dead in the eye, not fazed that she's topless.

"I want you to leave." I release her wrists and step around her.

She moves, and I hear the ruffle of the material. When I turn back, she's pulling her top back on. "Your father said you haven't been the same, and he's right." She lets her hand flitter in the air from the top of my head to my feet. "This... this isn't what I signed up for."

Does she think I'm insulted? "Then leave." I don't like that Alex and my father were talking about me.

Irritation tightens her features, but she smiles and takes a step toward me. "Fine. I get it. You have a thing for Layla. Right now, she's a new, shiny toy. So fuck her and get it out of your system, and when you are ready"—Alex reaches up and touches my chest—"we can get back to being grown-ups."

"Is that what you call this?" I ask, and once again, I have to remove her hands from me. "Us being grown-ups?"

Alex exhales loudly again. "After you grow a pair of balls and sleep with Frankenstein, come back to me."

I'm moving quicker than my brain can register. Alex screams as my hand tightens around her throat. "You fucking listen to me. You go near Layla, and I'll tell everyone about the whore you are."

Alex's face grows red, and I remove my hand.

The grin twists my lips. "I've cameras in this room with footage of you on your knees. I'll let everyone watch."

She rubs her throat.

"Get the fuck out of my house." I don't wait to see if she leaves, but I walk away from her. All I can think about is Layla. The day she left our foster home, she broke me. Since she came back into my life, she's destroyed what's left of me, and once again, I like the feeling of chaos.

***

I wake up to a text from Chester.

The package has arrived.

My clock reads three in the morning. Flicking on the light, I run my hands down my face while climbing out of the bed. Grabbing my jeans, I slip into them before picking up my jumper. I'm quiet leaving the house. I can't say the same for my BMW, but this meeting is too important to miss. This is what it's being all boiling down to. This one meeting would change everything. I will finally have the justice I seek.

Woodview Estate is in darkness as I drive slowly up to Chester's house. The curtains shift and light filters out before it gets swallowed up behind the heavy curtains. Killing the engine, I get out of the car and slide my phone into my pocket. The front door opens and Chester pops his head out.

Scratch marks down his face have me raising a brow as I move past him and into the house. The click of the front door closing has me glancing at him over my shoulder.

"What happened to your face?" I ask as he circles around me and pushes the sitting-room door open. We're the only people here. Every other time I've come to Chester's home, his crew has been hanging out here. Music plays quietly from a stereo close to the door. The bass sends a current around the room.

He sits down on the couch, and his bare feet shift back and forth as he rolls a cigarette. "That bitch, Ashley"—he licks the roll-up—"had a stranger babysitting my fucking kid." He places the cigarette in his mouth and lights it. "Fucking idiot," he mutters under his breath.

I sit down on the chair.

"No offense, bro," he offers up.

I relax my fingers and rub my palms along my jeans. "Why would I be offended? Do I look offended?" I smirk.

He shrugs and sinks back into the couch. "I know you have a thing for Layla, but she doesn't know my kid from Adam."

He has my full and undivided attention. I sit forward, resting my elbows on my knees. So that's who Layla was babysitting for. What fuck was she thinking?

"Ashley got you good." I take a quick look around the room. I don't see any gun or weapon near Chester.

"Fucking bitch." He takes another drag of his cigarette.

"Are we alone? I don't want anyone knowing my business." I don't want any witnesses.

He sits up, and his feet tap along the floor. "Nah, just me and you, bro. You want the goods?" His lip rises on one side.

I stare at him. We're alone. There's no one here to stop me. Should I ask for the gun first or hurt him first?

He gets up while crushing the cigarette in the large crystal bowl. "I'll be a minute." His smirk has me tightening my jaw.

"Did you frighten her?" I ask.

He stops walking and rubs his chin. He stutters a laugh. "She scares easily."

I get up. "Did you frighten her?" I'm no longer smirking. I'm trying to control the pure and undiluted anger that filters through my veins.

Chester licks his lips and shuffles from foot to foot. "I said the bitch scares easily."

My forehead connects with the bridge of his nose. The break is instant, along with the flow of blood. He grips his nose, and that gives me the perfect opening. My fists connect in rapid succession into his ribs, driving him back. Left, right, left, right. I dance the motherfucking dance, and he reels back onto the couch. He's howling. I turn up the music. The beat is fuel to the flames that are consuming me. I let it all go as I stand over Chester. He protests, but it doesn't last long as my fist connects with his face. My knuckles burn, but I don't slow. I make each hit count. He never gets one in, and the song finishes. Another one starts before I stop.

I'm breathing heavy. Blood coats the couch behind Chester's head. I can't make out his features as I gasp for air and my sanity. I think he might be dead.

I felt possessed. His hand twitches. One eye opens.

"You ever look at Layla again, and I'll come back and finish the job," I promise before leaving to wash his blood off me.

CHAPTER TWENTY

LAYLA (PRESENT)

I SWALLOW AS MY thoughts take a dive in a direction they have no right to go. His lips look... kissable.

How inappropriate.

"You're a sight, Layla." Jared's words carry a heaviness that has me swallowing. I brush some falling strands away from my face and get ready to get up.

"Don't. Stay where you are." Jared is with me in six large strides before kneeling. His red T-shirt clings to every defined crevice of his body. I swallow again, focusing on his jeans.

What's wrong with me?

He's watching me.

"What are you doing here?" I finally ask. I glance at the door again, only to find Carl observing us. He gives me a quick wave, which I return before he closes the door.

Carl doesn't look angry. After all, he said he wanted to meet Jared, and he did encourage me to go to the party. But I'm not sure what I saw on Carl's face. A part of me is happy that Evelyn isn't here. This feels like too much.

"He's a really nice man," Jared says. His brows furrow as he reaches for me. I freeze when he moves a piece of hair from my cheek before placing the lock behind my ear. The small bit of contact causes my breath to hitch.

"Yeah, he's the best," I manage to say. "Jared, what are you doing here?"

"I heard about what happened with Chester." Jared's gaze is heavy as he searches my face.

That's why he's here. Why am I disappointed? I'm not sure. I dig the trowel into the clay beside my thigh. "Yeah. Look, it's fine."

His tanned hand grabs my free hand, and even though it's gloved, I can sense his touch. His stare is unrelenting, and my breath stalls briefly.

"It's not fine. He will never speak to you like that again." My throat burns, and I drop my gaze, only for him to pull me toward him. I reach out, gripping his forearm to stop myself from falling completely into him. His grin has my heart stuttering in my ribcage.

His head dips, and a vise tightens around my chest. His grin grows, and his brown eyes are now flecked with gold. It's like he knows the effect he's having on me. My lips part as my heart accelerates into top gear.

Oh God, he's going to kiss me.

I need to stop this. When his forehead touches mine, the intensity I see in his gaze shocks me, and his grin is no longer in sight.

"He's an asshole."

My brain seems to short-circuit. *What? He's talking about Chester again?*

I lean back. "He's scary," I finally say, removing my gloves from my overheated hands.

"Did he touch you?"

The stare with which he pins me holds anger that has me immediately shaking my head.

"No, he didn't." I know I will never put myself in that predicament again. I wipe my forehead with the sleeve of my top. It feels like the temperature has jumped up several degrees.

He nods now, but no warmth has reentered his eyes. "It won't ever happen again."

"It's fine. How did you know about Chester, anyway?" I ask.

"He brought it up in conversation." Jared's jaw hardens.

"I'd like to know how that conversation went." I can't see Chester giving up the information, and right now, looking at Jared, I wonder if Chester is still breathing.

I've never seen such wrath in someone's eyes.

"You don't," Jared fires back.

Do I really care about Chester?

We sit in silence, and his gaze shifts to my plants. One of his brows rise in surprise. "So, you garden? And very well, I might add."

The change of topic has me sitting back. "Yep." I grin. "I try," I add.

Jared's head cocks to the side as a smile tugs at his lips. "You never could take a compliment." He examines the rest of the garden. There really isn't much to see. "Anything you touch blossoms. It always has." His tone drifts off as if he didn't mean to speak out loud.

"Thank you." My words are only a whisper, but he hears me as he looks at me with hooded eyes. Everything about him is so familiar, yet so new.

"You should really put down some membrane under the plants," he says, jutting his chin out toward the large, empty flower bed.

"Yeah, I will be. Since when do you garden?"

His smile turns into a full-blown one that has my heart skipping. "I have many talents, Layla." His double meaning has the tips of my ears turning red. His laugh at seeing me burn up nearly undoes me. I am so grateful when Carl arrives.

"Plants look great," Carl tells me with a soft smile on his face. Stuffing my hands into my pockets, I have to stop myself from bouncing up and down on the heels of my tattered shoes.

"I've four more to plant, and then I'm going to put wild indigo between every second one. They'll work very well together."

I can picture the garden when it's in full bloom; the off-white and lavender colors will blend beautifully against the gray slabs.

"May I help you?" Jared's question has me quickly looking at Carl, who's staring off into the distance.

"It's okay. I'm sure you have more important things to do," I answer him. Jared's mouth twitches like he's holding in laughter.

"Did you teach her how to garden, Mr. Masters?" Jared looks so confident with one hand tucked into his jeans pockets as he stands beside Carl. They're nearly the same height.

I have so many questions for Jared. First of all, *Mr. Masters?* How does he know their second names? And also, how does he know where I live? I narrow my eyes at him with suspicion.

Carl laughs, holding up his hands. "I wish I could take the award for that. But it's all on Layla."

"Not really. I wouldn't be able to do this if it weren't for you guys giving me free rein of your garden. Plus, you're paying for it."

The corner of Jared's lip lifts. "It looks like they made the right investment."

I blush at the compliment.

"It's a bargain, and we're grateful." Carl moves to me, kissing me on the forehead. The affection surprises me. "Okay, I'll let you kids get back to it."

Surprise fills me for the second time as Carl shakes Jared's hand before leaving. "Thank you for taking care of her, and I'm glad to have met you."

Jared's gaze flickers to mine before returning to Carl. "You're welcome, and thank you for taking care of her for me."

My breath catches at his words. Carl puts his second hand over Jared's, sandwiching it between his. I can't see Carl's face, but Jared's flashes with emotion. Carl gives their joined hands a final soft tap before turning to me.

I want to tell him how grateful I am for how he's treating Jared, how much it means to me. I hope he sees the gratitude in my eyes as he leaves.

I blink when the sliding door closes, only to find that Jared is watching me. I rock on my heels. "What?" I ask, wondering why he's looking at me like it's the first time he's seeing me.

His eyelashes flutter, and he's Jay again.

"So, what time will I pick you up tonight?" he asks.

I sit back down and pick up my gloves. I don't put them on, just hold them, and Jared sits down beside me, his shoulder flush with mine. We both face out toward my empty flower bed. He bumps into my shoulders.

"I've nothing to wear." Yeah, that sounded as lame as it did in my head.

"Wear whatever you want."

I glance at him sideways. "Fine, I'll wear my overalls."

His lip twitches. "That's fine by me. You look cute in your overalls."

I laugh at him. "Yeah. People will be dropping at my feet," I say, sliding on the gloves.

Jared's gaze drifts to me. He's focused, serious. "You're right. You can't wear your overalls." He grins now, not able to remain serious. "So, what time?"

My senses are committing to memory all these wonderful things about Jared: his smell, his smile, how his eyes light up, how he feels so right beside me. My pulse jumps along my neck as I focus on his lips. When I return his gaze, his pupils are dilated.

"I'm not sure."

My words have him blinking, and when he looks at me again, his eyes have returned to normal, and he stands up. "Great. I'll pick you up at eight. Wear something casual."

That's abrupt. I start to rise.

"Stay. I'll let myself out. Finish your planting." His face has softened again, and I find myself smiling at him.

"Okay, see you later." I watch him leave, spending a bit too much time watching his backside. I sigh and scold myself.

I stay out in the sun until I have all my plants in the ground. I need a shower, as I can feel the sweat dripping down my back. At the sound of the sliding door, I turn, expecting Carl, but it's Evelyn.

"How's my girl?" she asks. Her smiling face is like a hug. She spends most of her time happy. She's human, so she has her moments, but overall, she's a very happy person.

"I got the centerpiece finished." I stand up so I can admire my work as Evelyn joins me.

"Looks great. I hear you had quite the day." I glance at her to gauge her reaction, and her huge smile has me relaxing.

"Carl told you, then," I say, folding my arms.

"Yes, he did. He said Jared is very handsome."

Heat races across my face. I tilt my head slightly with a shrug. "I suppose." Handsome is an understatement.

"You suppose?" she says. I can hear the laughter in her voice.

"Yes, I suppose," I repeat and pick up my tools. "He has lots of admirers." I'm referring to Alex, who already staked her claim on him.

"And you have Kieran. That doesn't stop anyone from saying a person is attractive."

I cringe at Kieran's name. Ugh. I should have never lied. That's something I will have to come clean about, and sooner rather than later. But I'm not ready for that conversation.

"Yeah, I know. So how was work?" I ask, and I'm grateful when Evelyn allows me to change the conversation. I know we'll get back to Jared, and I'm okay with that, but right now, my body is filled with nerves as I think about the party tonight. Evelyn tells me about her day as we leave the heat of the garden behind us. We make our way inside the house, and the cold air hits me immediately.

"How are you feeling about everything?" Evelyn asks with her back to me. She turns and leans against the island. "I mean, is your sleep affected again?"

"No." I frown. "I toss and turn, but no night terrors."

Another gift of many that my upbringing gave me.

"I'm so happy to hear it." The smile that Evelyn wears is tight. The crinkles grow around her eyes.

"It was hard on you and Carl." The need to apologize has me brushing off imaginary clay from my overalls.

"Parenting *is* hard."

My eyes sting at her words. She says things so easily, like I've always belonged here. The truth is, my own parents didn't want me, so I was placed in the foster system, only to meet the worst side of life first. Jared, he was the light. The light in a world plunged and soaked in darkness and hate.

No wonder I ended up with night terrors. The small space I found myself in would grow tighter in my dreams. My hysteria couldn't be tamed.

Waking someone from a night terror is dangerous. I remember that when I would wake up covered in sweat, Evelyn would be awash with tears. The distress on Carl's face used to twist my heart, and each time, I feared they would send me back.

"Thank you for always being there, Evelyn. You and Carl."

Evelyn walks around the island, and I'm encased in one of her hugs. "Always, sweetheart." A kiss is pressed to my forehead, and I smile up at her when she releases me.

"I better wash up. I stink."

"I agree." Evelyn laughs as she steps away.

***

The spray of the warm water hits my back as I press my palms against the tiles of the shower wall. My mind throws me back into a haunting memory, and my heart starts racing. I squeeze my eyes shut, and when I open them, I'm staring at the white tiles. I focus on my fingers, spreading them out. I lift the pinky up before pushing off the wall and leaning back into the water.

Closing my eyes, I see him—smiling at me, his dimples on full display. His large, tanned hands appear so much bigger, and I run my hands across my abdomen, pretending they are Jared's. Flutters start low in my belly, and they spread fast and hard, leaving a throbbing between my legs. His kiss flares to life, and I lick my lips as if I can almost taste him on my tongue. My hand dips lower, and my teeth sink into my lip. I imagine Jared's fingers dipping inside me. I burn as I drag my fingers to my clitoris and rub it in a circular motion. The thoughts of Jared naked inside me rocks my body, and with very little effort, I release in the shower. I'm panting and a little stunned as my body jerks with pleasure.

I've come before, but it never felt like this. I've never had the reality of Jared all grown up, with his wicked words and deadly ways. I've never even tried to picture him as a man.

I stay under the water, and it feels like something inside me is changing, and I have no idea what it means. But a new want is rising inside me. I want Jared. That thought terrifies me.

CHAPTER TWENTY-ONE

JARED

I HAVE A SOUR taste in my mouth as I get into my car. I don't turn the ignition but look back at Layla's home. I don't know what I was expecting when I knocked on the front door, but it wasn't Carl, a man who truly loves Layla. He was genuinely happy to meet me. I came with the intention of confronting Layla for not answering her phone and warning her never to do that again. But as I stepped over the threshold, my intentions changed. Their home is modest, but it's a real home. I can picture Layla laughing here, eating, sleeping. I want to see her comfortable with her surroundings, and that's exactly what I found outside.

To see her kneeling, planting flowers, did something to me. Her eyes widened when she saw me, and I soaked up her surprise and stayed in for a while before finally sitting down beside her. With my shoulder so close to hers and the sun beating down on us, I found an odd peace that I've never felt. Each time she looked at me, I knew my father's words last night were lies. She didn't have it in her to deceive me. Layla is too good of a person. Too good for me. I should let her go. I should have listened to my father three years ago and allowed the idea of Jared and Layla to die. Everything she touches blossoms. Maybe deep down, I want her to do the same to me. I'm disturbed by that thought and leave abruptly, not wanting to dig any deeper. I have a plan, and Layla being here is making me question my plan to kill Bert. Before, I had nothing to lose. Now, I have everything to lose.

I turn on the car, knowing that letting her go isn't an option anymore. I drive straight to the gym. I'm thirty minutes early, but I don't think Rex will mind. Slipping my phone into my pocket, I get out of the car. Before entering the gym, I check my phone one more time. Rex isn't a fan of technology. No phones while training is another one of his policies. I have several missed calls from Alex. No messages. I place the phone on vibrate and grab my gym bag from the trunk of the car before going into the gym.

The smell is familiar, and it gives my mind instant permission to allow my body to relax. My brain seems to switch gears, and all that exists is here and now. Rex is in his office. The glass wall allows me to see him. He looks up from a stack of dockets, and I wave before pointing to the changing rooms. He salutes me with two fingers.

The locker room has recently been washed down. Rex doesn't have a cleaner, and he's too much of a perfectionist to hire one. So, I know this is his handiwork. I change into shorts and a T-shirt and return to the gym floor. He's no longer in the office but waiting for me by the main ring. I take his outstretched hand, and he half hugs me.

"Let's work on defense today." He speaks while releasing me and picks up the pads that are positioned on the edge of the ring. I pull on my boxing gloves and don't lace them up, as I won't be swinging any punches today. We enter the ring. We don't talk, and I'm in the zone, stopping every hit. I strike back a few times, only to have Rex reprimand me.

I grin. "It's automatic. I can't help it."

He's not amused. "You have to control your reaction. You know that. Shit like that makes fighters lose a fight. You have to keep your head in the match."

I slow down and drop my hands. Sweat soaks my body. We might not be full-on fighting, but we've been dancing around the ring. "I don't want to do any more tournaments." I know my winning fights gives Rex a large sum of money, but they just don't give me the same kick they once did. "I'll continue training and make sure my father gives a generous donation."

Rex waves me off. "I don't want your money, Jay. Your skill isn't something money can buy." Rex pulls off the pads from his hands. "What's brought this on? You have plagued me for tournaments for months, so why stop now?"

I have no idea why. *Layla.*

"My father wants me to take a more serious role in the family business."

Rex nods before running his hands through his hair. "I knew that would happen. I just hoped we had more time."

The gym door opens, and Warren O'Reagan steps in with a cigarette dangling between his lips. I'm waiting for Rex to have a fucking fit, but he doesn't say anything about the cigarette. Anyone else, he would have by the balls.

"We have assigned times here, Warren." Rex stretches the ropes and gets out of the ring.

I lean against the rope. "What's up?" I ask Warren.

"Jay," he greets. "I just need to blow off steam," Warren tells Rex. He isn't fazed as Rex continues toward him.

"Warren, I'm happy to have you here, but I don't operate like this. It's a one-on-one basis during training hours."

Warren looks at me. "I'm sure Jay doesn't mind."

This all feels like a déjà vu. I did this to Rex only recently with Lenny. I step out of the ring, wanting to make amends and not make this any harder on Rex.

"I do mind," I say to Warren. "I need all the help I can get from Rex. Hope that's okay."

Warren snorts before holding up both hands. "Okay."

"I'm not going to have to start ducking and diving from snipers, am I?" Rex is half teasing.

Warren takes the cigarette from behind his lips. "Nah, not really my style. I'll ring ahead next time." It's funny to see the level of respect in Warren's eyes toward Rex. I can't imagine Warren hears the word "no" very often. Warren gives a final salute while his cigarette ashes float to the ground. Rex and I watch him go, and I'm sure Rex is itching to clean up the ashes.

"You really think he'd hire a sniper?" I ask.

"He's an O'Reagan," Rex fires back before turning to me.

I know they're powerful, but to think they have that kind of power makes me pause. Having a friend who knows a sniper isn't something that comes around every day.

"I don't want you to give up on boxing, Jay. Just think about it." Rex gets back into the ring.

"I will," I offer before we start back into our training. My mind is made up about the competitions, but I don't want to end my time with Rex. I'll find a way to keep money coming to him. After all, in a few months, I'll inherit everything. I've never allowed myself to fully accept that I will have riches beyond anything I can imagine.

If Rex doesn't expect my money, then maybe I can help him find someone to fill my place. Maybe Warren might be the answer to that. Then again, I can't imagine him having any discipline. Time will tell.

The two hours fly by, and it's close to five when we stop. I'm soaked in sweat and take the bottle of water that Rex tosses to me.

"I have an old student returning. He's a cage fighter. I want you to come by one of these days and meet him." Rex isn't giving up.

"What's his name?" I ask.

"Max. He's a beast. Think Conan the Barbarian."

I drink half the bottle of water down. "You think I'd take him?"

Rex grins. "We'll see. I might let you spar with him."

I finish the water and hit the showers. When I'm redressed and leaving, Rex is back in the office, going through the stack of paperwork in front of him. Guilt causes a thickness in my throat. Me not fighting professionally will cost him, and I don't want to see him go into a bad financial situation. Maybe I can do a few more fights until he finds someone else. I wave to Rex as I leave the gym.

Throwing my bag into the trunk, I check my phone. I have two more missed calls from Alex. Worry worms its way through my system. She isn't normally persistent, but I've never turned her down before. I've never spoken to her badly either, and I've most certainly never put my hands on her. I push the phone into my pocket and get into the car.

When I get home, William has food ready for me. He follows our schedules closely, and at times like these, I'm grateful for that.

I take the sandwich and bottle of water upstairs with me. My hands are itchy as I hold the bottle of water under my arm and balance the sandwich in my other hand. I pull the key from around my neck and open the door, and the room bursts into light as I flick the switch. I make sure to lock the door behind me before I leave my water and food on the workstation.

I pick up one half of the sandwich and start to eat as I stare at Layla's face. I need to draw her in the garden. I need to capture that moment of her profile. Not seeing her fully didn't stop the contentment from showing on her face. I finish my food as I walk around the room, taking in all the pictures of Layla. She's so full of expression—each picture tells a story. In the one I stand before, her bottom lip is slightly pulled down, her eyes wide, and her hair rests on her shoulder.

She's staring at me with that look of hope and disbelief on her face. I continue to move along the images, and when I finish my food, I start to sketch. My hands take over as they move fluidly across the blank page. After an hour, Layla starts to take form on the paper. My phone buzzing in my pocket keeps distracting me. I check it, and it's Alex again.

It's also six thirty. Time is slipping away. I leave the room and lock the door behind me, then call Alex back as I place the key around my neck.

"I need you." She's been crying.

"What's wrong?" I'm moving faster. My mind jumps to the worst possible scenarios. Like she's being robbed, someone died, or someone really hurt her.

"Can you come over to my house?" Her voice doesn't hold fear, and I slow my footfalls.

I need to change for the party. "Can't you just tell me what's wrong?"

"Not on the phone, Jay." She snivels, but I can picture her rolling her eyes.

"I'll be there in twenty minutes." I hang up and get into a clean pair of jeans and a white shirt, then I pull a navy sweater over it.

***

Alex's home is a mirror image of ours, only hers is painted the ugliest peach, and the garden is filled with artificial plants. It looks flawless, but the smell is wrong. It's fake, like most of the people in her home.

I park outside the front door and not in the garage, as her parents insists everyone must do. I don't plan on staying long. The front door is unlocked, and I enter the foyer. I don't call out as I'm greeted by a member of the staff. She's a short, heavy woman who holds her hands in front of her. She's new, but Alex's family goes through staff members on a regular basis. I've stopped memorizing names at this stage.

"Mr. McGivney. This way, please."

I follow her to a sitting room that has the curtains drawn, and Alex is sitting on the couch looking the picture of an upset rich white woman. She has a crumbled-up tissue in her hand, her eyes are watery, and her lips are painted a stark red. Even in her distress, she still managed to put on lipstick. The room is lit by several lamps; the overhead chandelier hangs in darkness.

"What is it?" I'm irritated that I even have to be here. I check my phone. It's seven o'clock. I've one more hour before I need to pick up Layla.

She pats the seat beside her on the large gold couch. I'm ready to snap at her, but she blinks, and tears fall. I'm not a completely heartless bastard. I walk stiffly to the couch and stuff my phone into my pocket before I sit down. "What is it?" I ask again.

"My parents are getting divorced. I have no one else I can talk to about it." She gives a shrug of her shoulder that's bare; her white top has fallen down, revealing most of her left shoulder. Alex won't tell anyone about this. They'll keep it hidden. Appearances mean everything to them.

"I'm sorry, Alex." I have no idea what she wants me to say.

"I mean, I could expect my father to leave, but not the other way around." Alex blinks, and more tears fall. "My mother doesn't even want me. She didn't fight for me to live with her."

I feel the weight of her words and a sense of expectation that I need to tell Alex that her mother does want her. But maybe she doesn't—just like mine never wanted me.

"I'm sure your mother loves you. Would you want to live with her? What if she moves far away? What about your friends?"

Alex hiccups, and more tears fall. "I suppose they wouldn't be able to cope without me. But she should have at least asked me, Jay. Everyone thinks I'm some unfeeling and insensitive girl, when I'm just scared."

I've never seen or heard Alex so vulnerable, and it twists at my gut. "Look at me," I tell her. She does, and I feel like shit for my threat to her yesterday.

"I was an asshole yesterday. I shouldn't have spoken to you like that. But no one thinks you're unfeeling. Look at you." I reach out and touch a tear to make my point before dropping my hand.

"I wasn't fair either," Alex says. She doesn't look away from me as she dabs her eyes with the tissue. "You're forgiven." She smiles widely.

I'm aware of the time ticking away. "You'll be okay, Alex."

Her eyes fill up again, and she moves closer. "Can I have a hug?"

I hug her, and she buries her head in my neck. She doesn't smell like Layla. After a few moments, I break the hug. "I'd better go." I stand.

She's scrambling off the couch. "Could you give me a lift to the party?"

"You still want to go?" She doesn't look like she's in any state to go to a party.

"I won't let this drag me down." She forces a smile. She bounced back fucking quickly. My sympathy starts to dwindle.

"I'm sorry. I'm taking Layla."

Her mouth twists. "I don't mind. I'll sit in the back."

She's desperate. Alex not being the center of attention is something I've never seen her accept.

"Alex, don't," I warn as she makes her way to me. I can already see it in her eyes before she reaches up and places her hands on my chest.

"We are so good together."

I remove her hands. "I'm sorry," I say again. "I have to go."

"I'll find a way for myself, then." Anger fills her words.

I'm ready to leave, but I look back at her. "We *are* friends, right?"

She holds her head high and nods. "Yes." Her reply is filled with venom.

I've never thought about Alex in any way, really. She was always just there, and we played our roles that we knew we were expected to play.

"You're better than this," I tell her before I leave.

I hope she will see her worth and stop dancing to her father's tune.

I know I'm not playing this game anymore.

I know what I want.

That's Layla.

CHAPTER TWENTY-TWO

LAYLA

EIGHT O'CLOCK ARRIVES, AND the doorbell rings. My hand flutters to my white sleeveless shirt before grazing my knees. The rough material of the denim shorts scrapes the tips of my fingers. The see-through shirt material is light, and the cami underneath doesn't stop the cold air from touching my skin. Despite that, my temperature rises dramatically as the doorbell rings for the second time. My white tennis shoes sound loud as I walk down the hall. Taking one last look at myself in the hall mirror, I brush my hair back over my shoulder. My minimal makeup will work to my advantage as the night wears on, but seeing myself, I feel maybe I've made a mistake and should have applied a bit more.

The girl who stares back at me has large blue eyes that look wide with fear. Pulling my bottom lip between my teeth, I look away. It doesn't matter how I look; Jared is my friend—I grew up with him—and I need to remember that.

Within seconds of opening the door, I lose sight of Jared just being a friend. He's facing the road, his hands deep in his pockets. I'm snagged on the heavy black tattoo that encircles his wrist. I want to get a better look at it, but he turns, and his eyes flash before roaming across me from head to toe. I hold on to the door like it's a lifeline. His navy sweater fits him perfectly. As my eyes move higher, his Adam's apple bobbles, and I pass his plush lips before settling on the deep pools of his chocolate brown eyes. I pull my lip in between my teeth again. Jared's gaze flickers to my mouth. I release my lip immediately.

He stares at me, and I can't hold his gaze. I wonder what he sees when he looks at me like that. Am I dressed okay?

"You ready?" he asks. His brows furrow, and he turns slightly away from me. His change confuses me. Maybe it's the way I'm acting. I'm looking way too deeply into everything between us.

"Just let me grab my bag," I say as he steps off the porch.

"I'll be in the car."

I close the door and try to calm my erratic heartbeat. A squeal tears from my throat. "Oh, I didn't hear you."

"Just came to see if you were leaving. I wanted to say good-bye, and I hope you enjoy your night," Evelyn says, mirth in her voice, and she smiles. She hugs me, and I return the gesture. Her arms are so warm. She always runs a little hotter than most people. Carl often teases her, saying he should run a few pipes off her in the winter to heat the house.

When she releases me, I smile up at her. "Yeah, I just need to get my clutch." I pause before entering the kitchen to get it. "Evelyn, do I look alright?" I hold out the white shirt while chewing on the inside of my cheeks.

"You're beautiful, Layla. You're beautiful no matter what you wear, but tonight you look even more so."

Evelyn's words stay with me as I leave the house. Jared is in the driver's seat, his hands clutching the steering wheel as he faces forward, working a muscle in his jaw. I move around the car and open the door. Immediately, he releases the steering wheel and gazes at me. His jaw eases.

"I thought you changed your mind," he says as his lip twitches. His joking mannerism has me relaxing as I close the door.

"I was thinking about it, but the only way out is through the front door. So..." I clip my seat belt and glance at Jared.

His eyes light up with surprise, and his mouth pulls on one side. "Yeah, you wouldn't get away from me that easily."

I smile at his words. They make me happy, really happy. "I don't know, Jared. I think I could give you the slip." The deep laugh that erupts from his mouth as he pulls the car away from the sidewalk sends a shiver down my spine.

"We'll see," he says as his gaze bounces between me and the road.

After dropping my bag on the floor, I lay my hands on my lap. "So, where are we going?" I ask. It's something I've wondered all day since he left the garden.

He grins, and I'm grateful that he has to focus on the road. I use this moment to take in his profile. His jaw that twitches. I quickly look away, wondering if he's aware of me watching him.

"We're nearly there," he says after a moment.

I nod, but he doesn't see the action. "Okay."

"Don't be nervous, Layla." That surprises me. What makes him think I'm nervous? Then when I really think about it, I am nervous, but not about where we're going. No, it's how I'm feeling about him. "I won't let anything happen to you." When he says this, I have to look out the window. He still sees me as a victim.

"Yeah, I know," I tell my reflection. The night sky is a blank canvas waiting for the stars to appear. We pull off the main road and drive down a side road that's lit the whole way by small twinkle lights. They hang from every tree, and at the sight of them, I sit up and pay more attention to my surroundings.

A man in an illuminated jacket directs us to a temporary parking lot that's been set up on a beach.

"A beach," I say, staring out the window. Jared turns off the car, and my heart leaps as he takes my hand in his.

"Do you still trust me?" he asks, his eyes filled with raw emotion that causes my breath to hitch. I nod, and a slow grin spreads across his face.

"Let's go." He's out of the car and at my side in a moment. I pick up my bag as he opens the door for me. One hand is outstretched, and I reach out. My fingers look so small in his hand. He tightens his grip, and I'm not sure what to do. I keep waiting for him to let me go, but he still holds my hand as we walk down to the beach, our fingers entwined. Jared tugs on me, and I look up at him. His brows rise, and he has a silly smile on his face. This part of the beach is empty. A few people walk toward the larger gathering further down.

"Come on." Jared tugs me again, and he runs. We continue toward the water. We kick up the sand behind our heels. His large hand holding mine, the wind whipping past us, and the taste of salt on my lips is a moment of moments—one I will never forget.

When Jared releases my hand, I feel the loss immediately until I realize what he's doing. I copy him, tugging off my tennis shoes. I strip off my long blouse and dump my bag onto the sand. Jared has rolled his jeans up to his knees. I take his outstretched hand without hesitation this time, and we grin at each other before running into the water. This is us—we were thick as thieves as kids. Where he went, I went.

The cold spray hits me so hard that I'm laughing and screaming and running back to my pile of clothes. Large, strong arms wrap around my waist and lift me up into the air. The excess water that drips off me is freezing. I squeal as Jared pulls me back into the water.

"It's too cold!" I scream, and he dips my toes into the water. My mind goes to the lake, and the excitement leaves me. Then the heat of his chest against my back makes the whole thing feel different. He drops me lower until the water nearly touches my knees. I'm standing as the waves crash against my leg.

That's when I spot a star, the first one to show up on the blank canvas. Jared's arms hang close to my hips. I try to ignore the heaviness of them. Pointing to the star, I tilt my head back to look at Jared. "Make a wish," I say, and his nostrils flare as a tightness enters his jaw. My stomach hollows, and his hand touches my cheek—his brows furrow.

"I wish..." He pauses, and my heart drums.

"What are you doing?"

The warmth is gone. I only feel the cold, salty night water that laps against the back of my legs as I turn, along with Jared, to see someone standing near our pile of clothes.

"We'd better get back," Jared says, not looking at me. I'm surprised to find Kieran standing on the shore. His white shirt is light, nearly like mine, only his has sleeves. The shirt fits snugly against a surprisingly toned body.

"You're trouble, Layla," Kieran teases the moment I step out of the water. Jared tugs on his socks and shoes, not even waiting for his feet to dry.

"Yeah, a real troublemaker," I say, pulling on my shirt. Kieran laughs. Jared glances up at me. I can't get a read on him. He appears almost confused.

"I'm taking notes. Layla likes babysitting and water. You'll be a cheap date. I just need to find a baby."

I snort at Kieran. "I'm crossing babysitting off my list," I say.

He grins. "Amending notes. Only water on a first date."

Now I look away.

"She can't swim." Jared finally speaks, his words clipped. "Let's go, Layla."

Kieran looks between Jared and me, and I give him a tight smile. Jared picks up my shoes and bag, and I reach to take them from him, but he pulls back. I notice a red mark on the collar of his white shirt. I want to ask him where the lipstick came from, but he's looking away.

"I'll carry them." It isn't a statement, but a demand. Jared waits until I walk before falling in behind me. Kieran shadows me, taking each step with me.

"So, about that date," Kieran says, and I glance at him. He's attractive, with blue eyes and a cheeky smile. But I haven't forgotten how he was with Morgan the night of Chester's party.

"I don't really date," I say with a shrug. I can feel the full weight of Jared's stare on my back. This is like having a conversation with my dad behind me.

Kieran glances back at Jared, his brows pulling together before he turns to me, a smile replacing his frown. "Me neither. Hate dating."

I laugh at Kieran. He's persistent; I will give him that.

Up ahead, the party is starting to take shape. This isn't a regular beach party—a bar, DJ station, and even a dance floor have been erected. Most people wear white. Fire pits are spaced out and placed sporadically. The light from the fires doubles the shadows of all the people who stand close.

I notice some people sit on blankets. I'm about to mention not having a blanket but stiffen as Alex bounds toward us looking like one of those women from a Bond movie. Her gold bikini top is generously filled, water still clings to sun-kissed skin, and a flat stomach disappears under a long skirt that seems to flow across the sand. Her hair is wet and swept back. Drops of water hit me as she passes by. She stops at Jared, stretches on the tip of her toes, and kisses him softly on the cheek.

"Thank you for today." She sounds sincere.

I look away as my stomach falls like a rock. It's worse than the coldness of the water.

"No problem." Jared sounds stiff.

Alex giggles. "Oh, I got some lipstick on your shirt earlier."

Earlier? He was with her before he came to get me? My mind conjures up descriptive images of what they were doing.

I notice Kieran watching me, and I hope my emotions don't show. "I have a blanket if you need somewhere to sit," he says.

Yes is the right answer here. I need to leave Jared and Alex alone. But some part of me clings to Jared like a child to a parent's legs.

"It's fine. She can hang out with us," Alex says. She stares at him, blinking in rapid succession, but Jared is focused on Kieran so intently that I wonder what's keeping Kieran here. *Yeah, that isn't going to happen.*

"No, I don't want to intrude," I say.

Alex looks relieved.

"You're not. I'm the one who brought you." Jared finally looks at me, and I'm surprised that he can't feel the furious and beautiful female at his side. What is he doing? He clearly spent time with her before picking me up. The lipstick on his collar can't hide that fact. I have to stop this. He's trying to keep his promise that nothing will happen to me. His bringing me here is out of pity. But I'm not a victim anymore, and I actually, surprisingly, trust Kieran. He isn't a bad guy. Taking matters into my own hands, I gently take my shoes and bag out of Jared's hand. He resists at first but finally lets them go.

"I'll sit with Kieran. It's not fair leaving him alone." I turn to Kieran.

He gives me an easy smile. "Yep. If I'm alone, I may be attacked."

"Well, you kids have fun," Alex sings and reaches for Jared.

When Jared turns his gaze on me, I'm stunned to see so much anger in his eyes. "You aren't sitting with him." Jared's jaw is clenched, and this situation just went from uncomfortable to awkward.

My mind races, trying to make sense of his actions. One minute we're going to a party. The next, Alex, who really seems like his girlfriend, is here marking her territory. Now he wants me to join them—and something clicks. An unnatural stillness fills me, and I paste on a smile.

"I'll join you," I tell Jared, as if not joining him is an option.

I turn to Kieran, wanting to apologize, but he holds up both hands. "I'll leave you to it, but my offer still stands," he says, walking away.

I give him a soft smile before turning back to Jared. But It's Alex who I focus on, and the phrase 'if looks could kill' springs to mind. Yep, she hates me. But she has no need to. What clicked with me only a few moments ago is that Jared sees me as the young girl he spent his childhood protecting. For that, I will be eternally grateful. But I'm not a victim anymore, and after tonight, I'll have a chat with him and let him know he's off the hook. I don't need protection. The thought of losing him for a second time halts the air in my lungs.

Breathe. Just Breathe.

CHAPTER TWENTY-THREE

LAYLA

"L EAD THE WAY," I say before glancing up at Jared. A muscle tics in his jaw as his eyes cloud with sadness, which makes no sense.

I would have asked him what was wrong, but Alex tugs at his arm, getting his attention. "Come on. Mark's waiting for us," she says.

As I walk behind the happy couple, I glance over at Kieran, who's observing me. He gives me a wave, and I wish I were sitting with him. The idea of Alex and I in such close proximity is making my belly ache. But these are the people that Jared loves. Nothing is going to happen at a crowded party, and so far, Alex has been sociable. I need to be happy for Jared.

The fire pit that we stop at has several students I recognize from Kingscourt College. Alex accepts a kiss on both cheeks from the man she acknowledges as Mark. Mark's gaze finds mine, and he inspects me like I'm a fly he wants to squash. I'm sure Alex shared some delightful details about me. I think he was in gym class on my first day. Now that I really think about it, I'm sure he was there.

I glance around and focus on the friendly smile of Sam, Ashley's brother, who's at a fire pit across from us. I recognize the other boy who stands with him from my first day of class, but I can't remember his name.

"Layla, isn't it?" Sam asks as he makes his way over to me. His green eyes twinkle with alcohol. The smell of his breath brushes my face as he speaks. I can feel the heat of Jared on my left-hand side, and I know Mark is only inches behind me, along with Alex.

"Yeah. Sam, right?" I say.

His face opens up into a huge smile. "I knew I made an impression."

I nod before glancing over at Jared. He folds his arms across his chest, and my gaze snags on the band of ink tattooed on his wrist. Mark speaks to him, but Jared doesn't even look like he's present. He turns in my direction.

I swallow under the intensity. I want to ask so many questions. I've never felt so conflicted before. The pull that I feel toward him is clearly one-sided, but I still want to talk to him. I still want to relearn everything about Jared. I wonder what his life is like.

"Do you drink?" I ask, focusing on my words and not my emotions. Jared's lips part. Surprise flickers in his chocolate eyes.

"Yeah, I do."

He pauses before stepping closer to me. The world around us gets swallowed up, and it's just Jared and I.

"Are you going to tell me what you drink? Or do I have to guess?" I ask.

He smiles, dimples appearing, pushing my mind down the wrong path again.

Just friends. Just friends.

"Guess."

"He looks like a brandy kind of drinker to me," Sam says. That's when I notice everyone is listening to us. But I remind myself that we're two friends having a chat.

"Nah, I think Scotch," the other guy says. He has the same smiling green eyes as Sam. They are definitely related. They high-five.

"I wasn't asking either of you morons," Jared says.

"A beer?" I ask to erase the tension.

Jared's eyes light up, and his smile widens. "Nope."

I don't look at Alex or Mark, but their silence tells me they're listening.

Alex lets out a heavy sigh, one that can't be ignored by anyone. "He likes vodka and 7UP," she tells me with narrowed eyes before focusing on Jared. "That wasn't so hard, was it?" Her angry words are delivered with a shake of her head.

Heat filters across my face.

"You're being fucking rude." Jared's response is delivered with his own anger, and I want to dig a hole in the sand and disappear.

"No, Jared, you are. And after everything I told you." Alex's eyes fill with tears, and she takes a step away from Jared.

I have no idea what to make out of what's happening. My heart gives a heavy thud, and she runs off.

"You should make sure she's okay," Mark encourages Jared.

"I'll be back in a minute." Jared leaves, and it shouldn't hurt this much.

"She's very protective." Sam speaks beside me, giving me a kind smile.

"Well, when people stomp on your territory..."

My body freezes at Mark's words.

"Layla isn't stomping on anyone's territory," Sam says over his shoulder.

"I'm just saying. And who invited you to my party?"

Sam shifts uncomfortably. "You invited the whole college."

Mark looks Sam up and down with a sneer. "Oh, I forgot. Some of you are here on scholarships."

A group of girls approaches the fire pit and starts hugging and kissing Mark. He gets saturated with their affection and attention. They all walk away from the fire pit, leaving me with Sam and his friend. I'm wedged between the two.

"What a fucking dick," Sam growls after Mark and his friends. Mark can't hear him at this distance, but I nod my head in agreement. I want to look in the direction that Jared went, but I don't. He needs his time with Alex.

"So, how's my sister treating you?" Sam asks. His eyes sparkle. The darkness that clouded them only moments ago is erased.

"Yeah, she's great. Ashley's been really good to me," I answer honestly. Sam's friend leaves and heads in the direction of the bar; my assumption is to get another drink, leaving me alone with Sam. I just pray Sam doesn't leave. It'll look like I scared everyone off. Actually, I kind of have.

"Do you work?" I ask, wanting to keep him engaged in conversation.

"Nah, it's hard to get a job when you're living on my side of town." His words have lost the joking tone. He has been jovial since I arrived.

My gaze takes him in. He has on tracksuit bottoms and well-kept but worn shoes. The T-shirt he wears is clean but has that worn look to it. His friend arrives back carrying two red plastic cups. One, he hands to me. I take the cup and thank him. It will give my hands something to do. Sam returns to his joking way with his friend, who I find out is named Nathan. I relax, just listening to their banter back and forth. My eyes occasionally meet Kieran's from his own fire pit. He isn't alone anymore.

A dark-haired girl stands with him. He speaks easily to her, but she isn't leaning in toward him or doing anything romantic. They look comfortable with each other. My throat is dry, and I take a deep drink. The liquid soothes my throat immediately. I take another sip, liking how it's making me forget my problems and relaxing my body. When my cup is empty, I leave Nathan and Sam and go in search of the supply of alcohol. The bar is mostly empty. A girl with pink pigtails takes my outstretched red cup and fills it up. She looks like she's drinking more than she's giving out. Watching over the partygoers, I drink this cup slowly. My spine straightens as Mark materializes beside me.

"You're still here enjoying my alcohol?" he questions. He appears half-drunk, but awareness is still there.

"Yes, it's a great party," I say and feel a little surprised at my bravery. He smirks but with no humor. Mark's gaze takes me in from my bare feet all the way back up to my eyes before he walks away. I shiver.

I gulp down my drink and turn to the girl with pink hair. She seems even more drunk, if that's possible. I get half a cup this time as she sloshes the rest over her hand. As I glance around at everyone talking and laughing, I've never felt so alone. It's the worst kind of loneliness to be surrounded by other human beings, surrounded by noise, yet feel so insignificant. Even Nathan and Sam laugh about something I can't hear from this distance.

I look at the cup and make a decision. "Why not?" I speak my thoughts aloud and gulp the rest of the drink as I watch Kieran make out with the girl that I had assessed as a non-romantic friend. Yep, I have a great love radar. Just like I had with Jared, who enters the circle of light.

My stomach tilts when I see him across the beach. The light flickers across his face. He's looking for someone. Maybe Alex has returned too. I take another drink, only to find my cup empty again. Turning around to get a refill, I find no one is there to serve me. I reach across, turning the tap that's attached to a keg before filling up my cup.

"Hey."

I continue filling up my cup without looking at Kieran. "Hi." My greeting sounds sharp, electing a laugh from Kieran. I turn to him with narrowed eyes. "Why are you laughing at me?" I question him while taking another drink. Some reasonable part of me is saying I need to stop drinking and go home, but this angry part of me is growing and expanding, taking over every space inside my very drunk brain.

"Let's take a walk." Kieran takes my arm with a warm smile still on his face. He reaches for the cup, but I pull it out of his reach. "You've had enough."

My cheeks heat because I know he's right, but I drink nearly half the cup before handing it over. Then we head out across the beach.

The sand feels nice between my toes. The breeze tousles my hair. I glance down at our joined hands and focus on what I feel. Funnily enough, I don't mind his hand in mine; it doesn't cause the turmoil that Jared's does. I don't want to think about Jared like that. It just isn't right.

"Where's the girl you were kissing?" I ask.

Kieran kicks up the sand as we walk, and I notice he isn't wearing shoes either. "Not sure. Maybe she's off kissing some other guy." He glances at me.

The light of the fire pits is no longer our guide as we stroll down the coast. The moon, which is bright and high in the sky, shows us the way.

"Did you kiss any guys?" Kieran asks.

I burst out laughing. The sad reality is that I might have kissed guys before, but that's as far as it went. "No. I didn't get many offers."

He looks back at the sand, a smile still on his face. "I mean, I can change that."

I stop walking. "What are you going to do? Kiss me like you did the other girl?" I ask bravely. The drink is giving me a backbone.

"No. Never." Kieran lets my hand go and folds his across his chest. He wears the most serious look I have ever seen on him.

"So now you won't kiss me?" I continue on my very bold streak.

"I only kiss strangers. If I like someone, I'll take the time to get to know them."

I'm smiling, and Kieran smiles, too, while retaking my hand.

"You like me?" I ask, based on his logic of not kissing me.

He gives a short laugh. "I've asked you out several times. I thought that would let you know I like you."

"I just thought you were messing around." We've stopped walking again; I'm not sure why. But the moon seems to shine on Kieran like a spotlight.

His eyes roam my face as he speaks. "I was serious. Still am."

I feel grateful for his affection toward me, and I find myself taking a step closer.

"If I like someone, I kiss them," I say.

I watch as his lips part while his eyes flick to mine as I wet them.

I make a move, something I've never done in my life. The sad reality of my non-existent romantic life doesn't go beyond a kiss. My lips meet his soft ones. They feel warm against mine. My brain tries to make a comparison to Jared's. There is none. I hate that I'm even thinking about Jared. My tongue flicks out, and Kieran moans, pulling me closer to him. One moment I'm wrapped in his warmth, trying to push thoughts of Jared away, and the next, we're struck by someone. I open my eyes as Kieran is dragged and dumped into the water. The drink slowly fades as I race into the waves.

"Kieran!" Water splashes against my ankles as Kieran sits up, wiping water off his face. Jared stands over him. I can't see Jared's face, but I can tell he's breathing heavily from the movement of his shoulders, and before I can move another inch, he's reaching for Kieran again, and I'm running.

CHAPTER TWENTY-FOUR

JARED (BEFORE)

"I 'LL BE BACK IN a minute," I bite out, and I don't look back at Layla.

I search for Alex, but the drama queen has disappeared. I stop by the bar, and I'm ready to order a vodka and 7UP, but I think of Alex telling Layla that's what I drink, and I hate it.

"A beer." The red cup is filled from a keg. I expect the beer to be flat, but it tastes nice. I turn and keep scanning for Alex. I'll give her five more minutes, and then I'm going back to Layla. I finish the beer and see Alex with a group of girls who are squealing as they race into the water. They all huddle together as one of them snaps a photo.

Alex is smiling and laughing, her lips pursed for the photo. I'm wasting my time.

"Jay." The guy's accent has me turning away from the sea and toward the two guys who stand near the edge of the beach. Some underbrush has broken through the sand and taken over a small patch. I don't step closer to them. The tattoos that snake along their necks, and the small ones on their faces, mark them as part of Chester's gang. I knew he would send his men. I just didn't think it would be in such a public place.

"That's me," I answer while keeping a relaxed pose as I scan them for weapons. I don't see any, but that doesn't relax me.

"You've been issued your warning." He juts out his chin before taking a long pull of his cigarette.

"A warning for what?" I ask, dread tightening itself across my chest.

"You ever hear the term 'If you cut off a snake's head, eight more will appear'?" He doesn't wait for me to answer. Instead, he flicks his cigarette onto the sand; the amber burns brightly. "We're like that. You hurt one of us, and you have to deal with eight more."

I shift my stance, ready to fight. I grin. "You want to hobble home to Chester and join him with his recovery?"

My bravado is smashed as he grins back, like he knows something I don't. He holds up his fingers and makes the motion of cocking a gun.

"You fucked with the wrong people, bro."

I grin. "I ain't your bro."

The other guy, who has remained silent, slaps the fucker who still holds his hands up. He jerks out his chin. "Let's split."

He nods and drops his hand, but not before grinning at me. "Eight snakes," he says before leaving the beach, and it feels worse than anything. I need to watch my back. I don't regret beating the shit out of Chester. I made sure he'll never speak to Layla again. The delight I felt at breaking his bones was worth it. He isn't going to shoot me, but I'm sure I'll be jumped at some stage. I just need to make sure it's not when Layla is with me. I need to go to Chester again and issue him one of my warnings.

Hurting Chester has already cost me everything. The gun he was meant to supply me with won't be happening now. Killing Bert has been my focus for my months, my way out of this torture.

But I'll find another way.

I return to the bar with worry worming its way through my body. I don't want any repercussions for Layla. I can't let that happen. What if they hurt her? I'm turning away from the bar and making my way back to the fire pit where I left her. My fear almost consumes me when I return to find her gone.

Alex smiles at me sweetly. Water still drips off her body. She drinks through a straw while smiling.

"Where is she?" I ask and take a step toward Alex.

Her smile falters, but there's a level of satisfaction in her eyes that alarms me. "She went off with Kieran."

Before I can ask where, Alex points down the beach. I don't say a word as I take off after Layla. Please, God, tell me she's safe. If anything happens to her... I slam into a group of people, knocking them to the ground. Their shouts don't slow me down, and I race past the party, and the sounds fade away. I start to imagine what could be happening to Layla. What I don't expect is to find her kissing Kieran.

I don't slow down as I plow into him and drag him to the water, where I intend to drown him for touching what's mine. A thirst for blood drives my fist into his face, and I don't think anything could stop me, not even Layla's screams, as I plunge Kieran's head underwater and refuse to let him up. Madness drives me further as I watch him fight for air that I deprive him of.

He will never touch what's mine again.

CHAPTER TWENTY-FIVE

LAYLA

"**S**TAY AWAY FROM HER, or I will fucking kill you," Jared threatens.

Kieran's complexion loses all color. My heart thumps heavily in my chest as Jared's fist connects with Kieran's face. Kieran howls in pain, but his screams are cut off as Jared pushes him under the water. I've nearly reached them, and I keep thinking that Jared will let Kieran go, but he pushes his hands lower into the water, sending Kieran deeper.

"Let him go!" I push Jared with as much strength as I can muster, but he doesn't stop. "Jared!"

He looks at me, and it's like he doesn't see me. Cruelty darkens his eyes as Kieran swings blindly, struggling for air.

He's going to kill him.

My hands connect with Jared's side, but they make no impact. "Let him go! You're going to kill him!" I scream my fear, and Jared releases Kieran, who bursts through the surface, gasping for air while trying to get away from Jared. I reach for Kieran, but he moves away from me. He doesn't stop until he reaches the shore, where he falls to his knees.

I can't even look at Jared as I race toward Kieran. "Are you okay?"

He's still gasping for air, and when he looks up at me with angry eyes, I step back. "He tried to fucking drown me."

"Don't speak to her like that." Jared drags Kieran off the ground.

Fear drives my next words. "You're just like Bert."

It's like a blow, and Jared releases Kieran. This time, Kieran doesn't wait around. He takes off down the beach.

I've never seen Jared like this. I've never seen him so violent.

Jared is huffing, but he doesn't move. I want to take my words back because he's not a monster like Bert.

"You can't just do that," I protest.

"He was taking advantage of you." His eyes harden as he glances in the direction that Kieran ran off in.

"*I* kissed *him*, Jared," I whisper, not sure why I'm whispering.

Jared doesn't say anything for a moment; he just glares at me, burning away the last of the alcohol from my system.

"I can smell the alcohol on you. You're not thinking clearly." Jared takes my arm and leads me toward the party.

"I'm not a ten-year-old victim anymore." I pull my arm out of his hand angrily, and his eyes soften a fraction. "You keep looking at me like I'm a little girl." He seems to think I need to be saved.

He shakes his head while exhaling air from his body. "I definitely know you're not a little girl, Layla." The way his eyes roam my body as he speaks has sparks coming to life inside me.

"You need to stop putting yourself in bad situations."

Those sparks die a painful death. My eyes and throat burn. "Like what I did when I was twelve?"

Jared runs his hand along his jaw. "That's not what I meant." The silence stretches out.

"I didn't mean that about Bert."

Jared doesn't answer.

I fold my arms across my chest and glance down the path that Kieran took. "He's the first normal thing that's happened to me," I say, and as the words leave my mouth, I realize how accurate they are. He liked me. That was it. So simple.

Jared's shoulders are tense. His whole body looks like it's carved from stone. His eyes are a black abyss in which I think I might drown, so I look away.

"I'm taking you home. And don't argue with me." He reaches for me once again, but I pull away. "Layla." His warning has me moving.

"No. You don't get to tell me what to do, Jared. I mean…" The air grows heavy, and I wrap my arms around my waist. "I don't understand. You have Alex." I sound pathetic. "And that's fine," I add the lie.

Jared steps closer to me. "I don't want Alex."

I want to ask him what he wants, but a fear I've become accustomed to buries that question.

"I'll go home. But I wanted to go home, anyway." I turn away from him and start to walk back toward the lights of the party. Neither of us speaks. Jared stops by the fire pit and picks up my bag and shoes. Alex and Mark give me death stares. They don't ask Jared any questions. I use the moment to look around for Kieran, but he isn't at the fire drying off like he said he would be. I really messed up.

"Ready?" Jared asks.

I start walking—that's my answer to Jared. I take my bag from him as we reach his car. I wait for him to unlock the doors, but when the locks don't click, I look up at him to find him watching me.

"Even at twelve, you were never a victim. I have never met anyone as strong as you."

My eyes burn at his words. I never felt strong. I always hated myself for being so weak. My gaze flickers over the roof of the car to Jared, who places both his hands on top. I again notice the band on his wrist. His eyes burn with a conviction of his words.

"How can you say that? You had to save me every time." Jared blurs as my eyes fill up. Memories of Bert slapping me, closing his fist to me, kicking me, choking me, even spitting on me, come crashing back like a wave, and my body starts to shake.

I tuck my hands behind my back so Jared won't see the shakes that have taken over. "What's the tattoo for?" I ask to try to take the spotlight off me, but my voice trembles, and a tear escapes the tight prison I kept it in, trickling down my face.

Jared shakes his head as he moves around the car. His warmth envelops me, and I sink into his comfort, feeling like a coward once again. I always seem to need him. I think I'm starting to crave him.

Maybe I always have.

"Nothing will hurt you again." His hand moves through my hair so gently that I sense the touch down to my core.

"I'm sorry," I say, feeling embarrassed. I want to be strong. I need to be strong. But this isn't being strong. I swallow my emotions and move reluctantly away from Jared. His hands tighten on my forearm, keeping me from getting too far. I don't struggle or try to get away. Being here with him feels so right.

"I want you to listen to me." His head dips so I'm eye level with him. "Don't ever apologize."

I glance away, feeling my face burn.

"Layla." This time, the warning is different from only a few moments ago on the beach. It's strong, yet gentle. "You hear me?" Jared's eyes gleam like he's fighting back the tears, and that makes me pause.

"Yeah, I do. Are you okay?" I ask, and it breaks the spell. His violence toward Kieran scared me, and the look in his eyes now sends shivers skittering across my flesh.

He releases me and looks away briefly. When his gaze returns to me, his stare is empty, and I wonder if I imagined it only moments ago.

"Come on, let me take you home." He unlocks the car, but I stand there and watch him open his door. Our eyes collide once again over the roof.

"Get in, Layla," he says before disappearing into the vehicle. I get in but can't help that something niggles at me. For a moment, he looked so broken, and it's a look I used to see him wear when he thought no one was watching. But he was only a kid then. I never really questioned it, but seeing that look of pure devastation in his eyes makes my stomach tighten. I can't take my eyes off him as he reverses out of the spot, his arm behind my headrest as he looks out the back window.

"Why are you staring at me?" he asks, still reversing.

"I'm not sure. You just looked so sad a moment ago." Sad isn't the correct word. Brown eyes focus on me as his hand shifts the stick into gear.

"I hate to see you upset." Even as he says it, his voice holds a note of something else.

A lie?

"Why do I feel like there's something you aren't telling me?" I ask, and he zones in on the road with a laugh that doesn't sound real. It comes out more bitter than anything.

"Like what?" he asks as he puts his foot down way too quickly, jerking me forward. His arm shoots out to keep me from hitting the dash. "Put on your seat belt." He speaks through gritted teeth. He's like four seasons at once tonight. I can't figure him out. The snap of my seat belt has him pulling his arm away from me.

"Like how you're all emotional tonight." Emotional isn't the right word, but I don't know how to explain this.

"Yeah well, Layla, I just had a fistfight with someone..."

I sink back into the chair, my adrenaline crashing.

A fistfight? To me, it looked like Jared really wasn't going to let Kieran up. Another shiver assaults me at the thought. Maybe I saw it wrong. Maybe it was a fistfight. I forgot he knew Kieran. Are they close friends? My actions may have caused a rift.

"I'm sorry," I whisper.

His jaw twitches before he speaks. "It doesn't matter," he says, and I beg to differ, but I decide to leave it alone. Guilt eats away at me. I caused this. As I look out the window, I notice most of the houses are dark. Only one or two have lights on behind curtains. It takes us another five minutes of torturous silence before Jared pulls up to my house. The porch light is on. Bless Carl's and Evelyn's hearts.

My shoes sit on the floor of the car, and I unclip the belt while pulling them on. Sitting back, I grab my bag while reaching for the door.

"I never liked Kieran anyway, but he knew you had a drink in you."

I sit back and look at Jared, my mouth slightly ajar. His words are reflecting my thoughts, but I just nod, and Jared lets out a heavy breath.

"I don't want you thinking it's your fault." His hands clutch the steering wheel tightly. My suspicions are rising. "Same with Alex. That's not your fault either."

"Okay... Is someone going to say it's my fault?" I question slowly. Jared's gaze flickers to mine before he observes me. I want to squirm in my seat despite the heaviness of his stare.

"Yes. Alex will blame you, but it's bullshit."

Oh God, did she notice how I looked at him?

"Bullshit. You're not to blame," Jared tries to reassure me. But of course, he sees me as a friend and thinks that's how I see him. But Alex can see the truth.

"What did she say?" I whisper, not wanting to know but needing to.

"Stupid stuff that makes no sense." He shakes his head and releases the steering wheel. "Look, I'm exhausted. We can talk more tomorrow."

I swallow the fear that's clawing its way up my throat. Did I cause this? Is Jared too embarrassed to tell me what Alex said? I nod and open the door, one foot on the road, when Jared's hand circles my wrist. The heat of his hand warms the coldest parts inside me, and my eyes burn. I squeeze them before looking at him with a forced smile.

"We'll talk tomorrow," I say.

He studies me, his gaze making a pathway along my face.

"Good night." Two words, but it makes my stomach fill with lead.

"Night, Jared." He doesn't release my wrist, and I'm facing him again.

"I got the tattoo three years ago."

I glance down at his fingers that still encircle my wrist. Reaching out, I push the sleeve of his sweater up, and there it is, a dark ink band on his wrist.

"What happened three years ago?" I ask, looking at the smaller details on the band. It appears to be Celtic knots.

"I lost someone."

I look back up at Jared. "I didn't know. I'm so sorry." Shivers race up and down my arms.

"It's my handcuffs." His smile twists my gut painfully. He releases my wrist. "That's what it felt like. I was a prisoner in my own life."

My heart thumps heavier as he runs his fingers along his wrist, along the band of ink. "A reminder that this life would be torture without..."

I have no idea who this person was, but jealousy rears its ugly head, and I want nothing more than to find out who caused him such pain.

"Was it sudden?"

Jared's focus returns to mine. The haunted look leaves his eyes, and he sits back. "No."

I don't want to pry, but I can't help all the questions that flood my mind. "Was it family?" I ask.

His smile is bitter. "Yes, and No."

His mother? Ashley said his mother might be dead.

It's clear he doesn't want to talk about this, and I'm not ready to leave him. I search my mind for something to say. "I've always wanted to get a tattoo."

Jared's eyes widen with surprise, and both brows rise. "Layla with a tattoo," he teases. "What would you get a tattoo of?"

I shrug. "I'm not sure." An image of Tinnies springs to mind—happier times—and I use that humor to hopefully lighten this moment with Jared.

"Maybe a heart over my right breast."

Jared's laughter has me joining in. "Like Tinnies," he says.

My laughter starts, and it shakes my belly as I think of her. She was a large blonde Dublin woman with a heart tattoo on her right breast. She always pushed our faces into that breast while hugging us.

"Her boobs were so big." I nearly can't breathe with the laughter.

"She got off on it." Jared joins in, and when our laughter slows down, I realize how nice this is— laughing over the fun times. There was no harm in Tinnies.

"What was her real name?" I ask.

"Not a clue." Jared sighs like he's content, and I wonder how long it's been since he's laughed. I think of the look in his eyes earlier, and it dries up all my humor.

"You know, I'm here if you need to talk."

"Yeah, I know." Jared reaches across and touches my cheek tenderly. "Now go to bed before I change my mind."

I want him to. "What will happen if you change your mind?"

He releases my face. "Don't, Layla."

I want to poke at him, but instead, I lose any semblance of bravery and exit his car.

CHAPTER TWENTY-SIX

LAYLA

I WAKE UP SUNDAY morning to a message from Jared.

I'm sorry for being a dick last night. I was out of order. Can I make it up to you?

I smile at his words. Even after so much time away from each other and after his argument with Alex, he's still here for me. Thinking of him not dating Alex gives me way more joy than it should. I'm still unsettled with his violence toward Kieran. I have no idea how he is. Maybe it was just a fistfight between two guys. I had a lot of drink, so I may have judged the situation wrong.

Sure, what do you want to do? I type back quickly and leave the phone on the bedside table as I enter the bedroom and wash my face and brush my teeth. I hear movement downstairs, and I can smell breakfast. The crispy bacon has my stomach grumbling—the scent is divine. I leave my bedroom and make my way to the kitchen.

Evelyn is waiting in the kitchen with a plate of toast on the table. I go straight for the coffee, my head complaining about all the alcohol I drank last night. Evelyn doesn't say anything until I sit down. Instead, she butters a slice of toast and cuts it into triangles, then piles bacon on my plate before passing it over to me.

"I know we haven't put down any ground rules, but I think we should."

A flush creeps across my cheeks.

Evelyn immediately waves her hand at me. "I'm not reprimanding you, sweetheart. It's just that I worry."

I take a bite out of my toast to give myself something to do. "No, I get it."

Carl arrives in the kitchen then, with a gray suit on, his face freshly shaven. He's leaving on another business trip. He kisses me on the head before moving quickly through the kitchen, gathering up his travel mug, keys, and phone.

"Fun night?" he asks while looking for something else—most likely his wallet, which he always leaves in the woven basket on the hall table.

"Yeah," I answer as Evelyn watches me. A soft smile tugs at her lips.

"It's in the basket in the hall," I tell Carl.

He finally looks up at me, his eyes lighting up. "You're right." He gives me another kiss on the head before kissing Evelyn softly on the cheek. "I'll see you girls tomorrow night," he says before leaving.

I chew on the toast as Evelyn drinks her coffee. "I think we should limit ourselves to three drinks."

I nod immediately. I'm not one for drinking anyway, so I won't be repeating last night again.

"How do you know I had more than three?" I ask.

Evelyn grins. "Have you looked in the mirror? And I was your age once."

I haven't looked in the mirror, but I obviously look terrible. I'm about to comment on the age thing, but the doorbell rings. Evelyn gets up to answer the door, and I wonder what Carl has forgotten this time. He's always leaving something behind. I break up the bacon and put it on my toast.

I can hear the front door close. "What did he forget?" I call. I look toward the door, and there's Jared, looking so out of place in my home. He towers in the doorframe.

"Jared! What... Why are you here?" I ask.

Evelyn steps up behind him. She tilts her head so I can see her and widens her eyes. Humiliation stains my cheeks as Jared steps into the modest kitchen. He sits down beside Evelyn's chair.

"Don't be so rude. He's obviously here to see you," Evelyn tells me.

My humiliation triples.

Before I can reply, Evelyn speaks to Jared. "Tea or Coffee?"

Jared watches Evelyn, and there's something in his gaze that I can't decipher. It's not like the way he looked at Carl. With Carl, I saw respect; I saw a relaxed Jared. Right now, he seems guarded.

"Tea, please. Thank you, Mrs. Masters."

Evelyn's about to pour his tea, but she pauses with a smile on her face. "Call me Evelyn. Otherwise, you will make me feel like an old woman."

"Thank you, Evelyn." Jared's voice is smooth.

He glances at me, and his lip quirks up. A dimple erupts on his cheek, causing my heart to falter.

"Every time you see me, you make me feel so unwanted." His teasing tone has a chuckle coming from Evelyn. I'm trying to take in that Jared is sitting beside me in my kitchen as Evelyn makes him tea. Then I remember I'm in my bedclothes, and after Evelyn's statement, I more than likely look like someone who has a hangover.

"You keep arriving unannounced," I say in my defense.

"You never answer your phone."

I narrow my eyes on him. He has a point. I left my phone upstairs, but his arriving unannounced still rattles me.

"Here, sweetie," Evelyn says as she places the mug in front of Jared. Evelyn sits down with a raised eyebrow at me. I know that look she's giving me. It's to mind my p's and q's.

"So..." I say to Jared, whose eyes light up gleefully at my discomfort.

"So…" he says before taking a sip of the tea, dragging out my torture. "I'm here to take you out."

My face heats. Thankfully, Jared focuses on Evelyn. It gives me a second to try to gather myself. Instead, my eyes roam over him. His gray T-shirt fits him snugly. Tanned arms rest on the table. The tattoo sends the small hairs on the back of my neck to rise. He lost someone three years ago. Maybe one day he'll trust me enough to share more with me. My gaze follows the curve of his neck and across his sharp cheekbones.

"This tea is great. Thank you," he tells Evelyn, making me look up to find her watching me. She glances back to Jared.

"You're welcome. So where are you thinking of going?" The question isn't asked with the recent joking nature that she's taken since Jared arrived. She sounds like a mother. What has changed?

Is it because she caught me looking at him?

"To my house," he says before looking at me. "I thought you might like if I showed you around our gardens."

My heart swells in my chest. When I glance at Evelyn, she's hiding a smile behind her mug.

"Yeah, sounds great. I'd love to see your gardens," I tell Jared, and he lets out a little breath like I might have said no to him. I'm beginning to learn that saying no to Jared isn't exactly an option.

"Whenever you're ready."

I wonder if today is because of last night. Does he feel guilty about Kieran? He's here because he cares about me. Because I'm his friend. Right now, I want to hug him. Jared tips his head to the side. "You okay?"

I've been staring at him for far too long. My gaze snaps to Evelyn, and I get up to try to hide my embarrassment. Yeah, she's amused by it.

"Yep. I'll go get ready." I don't look at either of them as I leave the room.

***

The blue sundress makes my already large blue eyes pop. It's my favorite—the one I keep for special occasions. But I rarely get to wear the dress. I only wore it one time, when Evelyn's sister's son was being deployed, and we had to attend the 'final meal.' That's what Carl called it once we got out of the house. I hid the grin, but his wink told me he saw my smirk. It was the most depressing meal I've ever attended, and I had so many shitty dinners with Bert and Ronnie that I didn't think anything could be worse. I was wrong.

Evelyn's sister, Rose, looked nearly identical to Evelyn and spent the meal sobbing onto her fork, which she would fill with food, push into her mouth, and then cry on. The fork would remain locked between her lips. It wasn't until her husband comforted her that she removed the fork and chewed her food slowly and loudly. The son—I can't even remember his name; Scott I think—ate his food mechanically, and every once in a while, he would glance over at us and apologize before patting his mother's hand.

My fingers run down the buttons on the full length of the dress. Giving myself one final look in the mirror, I flip my hair back over my shoulders.

As I approach the kitchen, I can hear Evelyn's and Jared's voices. They chat easily; the topic is the weather. Once I open the door, my stomach flips as Jared turns toward me. A slow smile spreads across his face, and his dimples appear. I stop at the door, trying to calm myself.

"You should maybe grab a jacket." Evelyn's voice pulls my attention from Jared to her. Her eyes say so much more, like: *maybe grab some common sense while you're at it*. I get my jacket and bag off the hook in the hall as I talk to myself. "I need to pull myself together." When I return, I'm more composed and smile at Evelyn. "I shouldn't be too late," I tell her.

"Have a good day." Evelyn gets up.

"I've got it from here," Jared says while taking my elbow. Something in the way he speaks to Evelyn leaves me uneasy as he escorts me out of the house.

"Was there a problem while I was getting dressed?" I ask as Jared opens my car door.

"No problems. Why?" He grips the door, and I'm not ready to get in.

"If there were, you would tell me, right?"

"There is no problem, Layla. Get in the car." He says the last part with a slight grin.

I slide into the car, and he closes my door. Jared gets in, and I'm consumed with his scent.

"So what do you think?" I ask as Jared starts the car, and we take off. It's warm, and I roll down my window.

The slight breeze that floats in cools me down nicely.

"I have AC," Jared says with a smile in his voice.

"I know. I like the natural air."

"I think you look beautiful."

My heart pitter-patters at his words.

"I can't stop thinking about fucking you," he continues.

The saliva in my mouth feels heavy, and I swallow it with a bit of trouble before coughing. Why would he say something like that? Did I hear him wrong?

"You keep saying that."

He looks at me, his eyes dark. "Because it's true." His gaze roams down my body.

He confuses me. My mind goes to a place where Jared's hands are on me, and the hairs rise on my arms.

"How?" I whisper.

"How would I fuck you?" Jared doesn't hold back.

I realize I'm not ready for this conversation. "When I asked you what you thought, I was referring to Evelyn. What did you think of her?" I hope moving to safer ground will cool me down. I push the window down a bit more and have to grab my hair as it whips around my face.

The natural air stops, and a blast from the AC has me releasing my hair as Jared rolls up my window.

"Talking about Evelyn in the same conversation about me fucking you seems a tad bit inappropriate." He smirks at me. "Don't you think?"

I try to open my window again, but it's locked. "That's not fair," I say to the window.

"You can't run, Layla, or hide."

I look back at Jared. He's enjoying this too much.

My heart races. "I've never been with anyone." My face blazes as the car swerves slightly before Jared gets it back on the road.

The blood roars in my ears. I shouldn't have told him that, because it looks like I'm thinking about sleeping with him. Which I am.

"Like *dated* someone?" Jared's mouth is slightly ajar; his brows drag down. He keeps looking at me.

"Focus on the road!" I bark, and he switches his attention from me to the road.

"Layla, answer me."

"No, Jared, not like dated!" I don't know why I'm shouting.

He keeps looking at me like I've just materialized out of thin air. He refocuses on the road, and when he looks back at me, I see the truth settle in his mind. "You're a virgin?"

I hate that word. "Yes."

I don't want to look at him. I'm sure he won't want to touch me now. That thought is crippling.

"That's perfect."

My gaze snaps up to him.

"You're perfect." He's speaking to the road, but he finally looks at me. "It will make each second even more enjoyable."

I swallow at his words, and the funny thing is, they excite me. Jared doesn't ask why I'm a virgin. He doesn't seem to think I'm broken or that I must have some damage on my body. He knows every part of me. I find myself reaching for my scarred leg.

"You're fucking perfect." His words are harsh. "Every single part of you." He reaches toward me and touches my face.

I could get used to his words. I nod. A sense of being overwhelmed at his compliments flood my body.

He releases my face, and we stop outside his house. The thought of being alone with him is frightening but exciting too. I keep stealing glances at his profile as the gates open, and he resumes driving up to his home.

"So, what did you think of Evelyn?" I ask, trying once again to move our conversation to more comfortable grounds.

"She treats you well?" he asks.

It's not the response I want. But I answer his question. "Yes."

"You love her?" He shifts the car into drive and pulls into a garage.

"Yes, I do," I answer easily.

"She loves you too?" Jared looks at me after killing the engine.

I find myself smiling. "Very much."

"Then I like her," he answers.

His gaze burns deeper than anything I've ever felt before. It sends electricity racing through my body. "A virgin."

"You make it sound like I'm going to be a sacrifice," I try to tease.

Jared leans closer. "I mean, ropes and candles do sound nice."

My face blazes. I'm not naïve, but the thoughts of Jared like that make me see him differently.

Jared smiles. "Don't look so terrified."

"You're joking." I let out a heavy breath and try to calm down.

"No."

I'm waiting for him to laugh, and when he doesn't, I have no idea what to say.

Jared gets out of the car. "Let me show you the gardens."

Right now, I don't care about the gardens. I get out of the car and follow him out of the garage.

Ropes and candles.

"I'm just showing you the gardens. You look ready to run." Jared's teasing tone surprises me, and when he reaches back, I zero in on the ink on his wrist before taking his hand, and my soul sighs.

It's like I'm finally where I belong.

CHAPTER TWENTY-SEVEN

JARED

S HE'S A VIRGIN. THE more I get to know Layla, the harder I fall for her. She couldn't get any more perfect. She's mine and no one else's. She will be willing to learn with no preconceived notions. My fingers tighten possessively around hers.

"You own all of this?" Layla asks, looking around. I've never given much notice to the gardens, but Layla makes me see the vast space differently.

"Yes." Privileged. That's what I would have said when I stood on the other side of money. This is a life of privilege. Funny how it's never felt that way. I've always felt like I don't belong in this world. I belong with Layla. I'm tempted to tighten my hold on her, but her hand is fragile in mine.

"It's beautiful. It makes my garden look pitiful." She's half laughing, but I don't like when she belittles herself. I don't like it one fucking bit.

"Landscapers did this. It's not a labor of love like your garden. I'd prefer to sit in yours with you than here."

Her laughter dies, and she smiles at me. "Well, here we are. Alone." Her cheeks heat.

"Yes, we are." I stop and pull her closer. I still hold her hand in mine as she looks up into my eyes. Her lips are the most perfect shade of pink I've ever seen. Her blue eyes swim with a want that I'll gladly satisfy.

I press my lips against hers. The warm and moist feel has my cock growing instantly. Releasing her hand, I grip her face to drag her closer. Her lips move under mine, and I smile into the kiss. She's a quick learner. The memory of her kissing Kieran has me pressing harder on her lips, trying to erase the image. My tongue darts out and quickly fills her mouth. I release some saliva onto her tongue and break the kiss, wanting to leave my mark in her mouth. I feel satisfied when she swallows. She looks uncertain, and I don't give her time to think about what I just did. Gripping her hand, I keep us moving until the orchard starts to take shape. I had William set up a table and chairs in the middle of the orchard. Food covers the top.

"Wow." Layla takes it all in, and I watch her. She's so fucking perfect. The thought of grabbing her and fucking her on the table has me releasing her hand.

"Are you hungry?" I ask as I step over and pull out a chair for her.

"You didn't have to do this, Jared. It's too much."

I pick up a plate and stack it with a little of everything. William didn't hold back. "I didn't. William did."

I pass the plate of salad, cucumber sandwiches, and a selection of cheeses to Layla. Opening a bottle of red wine, I pour her a glass before filling one for myself. My chair is positioned at the opposite end of the table. I take a gulp of wine while picking up my chair and bringing it closer so I'm seated right beside Layla. She glances at me from the corner of her eye. Once I'm seated, our thighs brush the other's.

"Are you not eating?" Layla asks.

I pick up a sandwich and take a bite. "Satisfied?" I ask.

She picks up her own sandwich and nibbles on it. I love how her mouth moves around the food. I finish mine and sit back, just taking her in. It's like magic that she's here drinking wine with me.

"I never thought I would find you," I admit.

I like watching her reaction to everything I say. She's so filled with expression. She tilts her head, her drink halfway to her mouth. She's breathing a little heavier. "I never thought I'd find you, either."

I glance down at the glass that I hold, seeing the inked band on my wrist that still feels relevant, even though I found her. "I got this tattoo because of you."

Her eyes widen, and she places her glass on the table. "I don't understand. You said you lost someone three years ago. We've been separated for seven."

"You've been keeping count," I joke, but the humor doesn't drop. "Three years ago, I came to the conclusion that I wouldn't find you." Half-truth. Three years ago, my father told me to bury the notion of Layla and Jared. Three years ago, I became a prisoner in my own story.

Layla reaches out, and her fingers trace the band on my wrist. "I don't think a day has passed that I didn't think about you. The first few months"—she shakes her head—"nothing made sense. I kept thinking something inside me had finally broken, but I couldn't explain it. I've never felt whole, Jared." She blinks and tears fall.

Her words hit me so fucking hard.

"But I do now." She's smiling through her tears.

I tilt my chair further so I can reach her and pull her closer. I lean my forehead against hers. I wish I could tell her the same, but sometimes I still feel so dead inside. I know why. My gut clenches, and I refuse to acknowledge every emotion that slams into me, demanding my attention.

I half stand. My mouth finds Layla's, and when she moans, I pull her out of the chair without breaking the kiss. My cock grows hard, and this emotion I allow to fill me up feels like lust, but so much more. It consumes me. I run my hand across the table. Plates of food clatter to the ground and smash, but I don't give a fuck as I grip Layla by the waist and lift her up onto the table. I drag her to the edge, and her breath halts as I push my erection close to her opening.

I want to be patient, but there's a roaring demand in my mind that I take what is rightfully mine. My kiss grows savage. My fingers work on the buttons of her dress. Her small hands push against my shoulders, and somehow, she manages to pull her mouth away from mine.

"Jared, wait." She's panicked and breathless.

I don't move away as I fight for control, but I stop and allow her a moment to breathe. My gaze meets hers. "We're outside in the open. Someone could see."

"No one is here." It's a lie. The staff is here, but I don't care if they see. I've never wanted anyone so badly. I slowly hike her dress up past her knees, dragging my hands along her warm flesh. I pause and allow her a moment to stop me. I don't break eye contact as I continue to push the dress past her thighs. I release it and let my fingers trail across her flesh.

She tries to pull away when I touch her scar, but I don't let her out of my hold as I continue up her legs. Her fingers dig deeper into my shoulders. Her gaze clouds as I make my way to her panties. Gripping either side, I shift them, and Layla lifts her bottom so I can drag them down her legs. My erection strains painfully against my jeans as I pull her white thong down. Once it slips over her feet, I take the fabric and push it into my pocket. She watches me and doesn't move as I press my hands against her thighs. Her breath hitches as I drag her closer.

"I want to taste you," I say.

She nods.

Bringing her to the edge of the table, I bend down and press a kiss to the inside of her thigh as I part her legs. She exhales loudly at the contact. She smells perfect; her arousal and natural scent are heavy between her legs.

My mouth finds her pussy. I suck her clitoris and let it go abruptly. Her hands sink into my hair, and she hisses in shock. I don't give her a moment to recover before running my tongue along her clitoris and down to her opening. She's wet, and my cock throbs painfully. I want to bury myself inside her sweet pussy. My tongue sinks deep, and I taste her. I swallow her juices before releasing my saliva across her clitoris, making my mark again. Her fingers tighten on my hair as I press a kiss to the inside of her thigh before looking up at her. Her hands slip to my shoulders, and she appears disoriented and breathless—a perfect combination.

I slowly pull her dress back into place. Her mouth opens and closes, and her brows drag down.

"I just wanted a taste." I lean in and press my lips against hers. "You taste fucking perfect."

The agony in her eyes for more makes every passing second a pure pleasure. I'm the only one who can take that agony away. I'm not ready to do that just yet.

"Let me show you the rest of the garden." I grip her waist and lift her easily off the table. Once she's standing, she glances around her like she has no idea what's going on. The table is a mess, the ground coated in broken plates.

"We should tidy up." She's already flushed, but her face grows redder. I take her hand, making her look at me, and pull her away from the mess. "That's why I have staff."

She looks back at the broken plates, but she has no choice but to go with me. I reach into my pocket and touch her panties, making sure they're safe.

"I need my underwear back." Layla's gaze snags on my pocket, and I grin.

"I'm not done with you yet," I say.

Pleasure dilates her eyes, and I stop and kiss her again. I don't make the kiss long—just long enough to keep her blood heated.

I continue through the garden, identifying the different areas. I don't think Layla takes in a word, and I'd laugh, only my cock hasn't softened. It's like a lump of steel in my jeans. We reach the destination I had in mind. A small courtyard hidden behind the gardens comes into view. Its open walls and huge roof keep the cushion furnishings dry. The area is surrounded by large palm trees and an array of potted plants. It's the most secluded area in the garden.

We walk through the rows of vegetables, and Layla looks around like she's interested, but my erection keeps dragging her gaze to my jeans.

I stop walking as we approach the courtyard and spin her so she's facing me. Her breathing grows frantic with anticipation, and it's fucking delicious. I reach out and unbutton her dress further. Her breasts fill her white bra, and I push aside the material, exposing her breasts. She reaches up to cover herself, but I stop her.

"I want to taste you," I say and hold eye contact.

She nods.

I bend my head and suck on her rock-hard nipple. My trousers grow damp with precum. Moving my mouth to the other side, I suck on her nipple before grazing the sensitive skin. She hisses in pleasure. My own composure is slipping as I slide my hand up her leg. Layla's pussy is wet, and my fingers easily slip inside her. She gasps.

Releasing her nipple, I look up at her, wanting to see her face as I push two fingers inside her tight pussy. Layla's eyes are closed as she moans. Her hands tighten on my shoulders, and I wonder if she's going to come. Removing my fingers has her eyes snapping open, and I see the delicious torture there.

I wrap my fingers around hers. "Let me show you the courtyard," I say, and Layla stumbles as I tug her. When I glance her way, I can see the annoyance and frustration hardening her features. Yet, she won't voice what she wants.

"Is there something wrong?" I ask.

"Nope," she bites out, and I grin.

"If something is bothering you, just tell me." I step up onto the wooden platform that has a tiled roof. The L-shaped couch will really let me spread Layla out, but I want her to be comfortable enough to ask for it.

"Nothing." She exhales. "It's beautiful here."

I release her hand and remove her panties from my pocket. Her cheeks flame.

"I'll give you a choice. You can take your panties back and put them on, or I can put them in my pocket and finish what I started." There really isn't a choice. I am going to taste her ecstasy on my tongue either way.

She reaches for her panties, but her hand drops away. Her pulse flickers in her neck. "I want you," she whispers.

I stuff the panties back into my pocket and erase the distance between us. I reach for her dress and unbutton it further until I can push it down her shoulders.

She's looking around us.

"No one can see," I whisper as I brush a kiss to her earlobe before pushing the dress down until it pools around her feet. I get a glimpse of her pussy, and my cock throbs. I lean in and steal a kiss while I unclip her bra. The straps slide easily down her arms, and I capture a nipple in between my thumb and forefinger. Her head rolls back as she moans.

Watching her is a new kind of pain that I know I could become addicted to. I continue to play with her nipple before pressing a kiss to the pulse on her neck. Her earlobe is warm in my mouth as I suck the soft flesh before I pinch her nipple. Her groan has me guiding her back to the couch. I don't have to tell her. She sits at the edge of the L, and she lies back.

My balls are heavy, and the torture of spreading her legs and not sinking my cock inside her has me groaning. Wetness gleams off her inner thigh, and when she sits up, she looks delirious.

I don't keep her waiting any longer before I dip my head and bury my face in between her legs.

"Oh my God." Her words and groans have me sinking my tongue inside her. Her hands are heavy on my head as she shifts, and when she puts pressure on me, I'm good with burying myself deeper in between her legs. I lick her clitoris and suck it until she's squirming under me. Her pants grow frantic, and I consider stopping so I can watch this all play out. I must have paused.

"Please, don't stop." She's breathless, and her plea is music to my ears.

I reach up and dip two fingers inside her as I race my tongue up and down her clitoris.

"Oh God. Oh God." Her pleasure heightens, and I move my fingers quicker inside her. Her pussy is tight, and I'm tempted to add a third finger, but she starts to tremble as I lick her faster. She comes hard on my tongue, and I swallow as much as I can as I remove my fingers and lap up every single drop of Layla.

CHAPTER TWENTY-EIGHT

JARED

S HE'S BEEN QUIET EVER since I made her come. I want to do it all over again. She's walking aimlessly around the courtyard. It's clear she's frazzled. I enjoy sitting on the couch and watching her. She repeatedly glances toward me and pauses before she starts walking again.

I'm entertained, but my cock is painfully hard. I sit forward, placing my elbows on my knees. "Has anyone made you come like that?" I ask.

Her cheeks heat. My suspicions are confirmed. Her experience is far more limited than most nineteen-year-old girls.

"It's okay. It just means you have a lot more to experience." I push off the couch. Her hands instantly go behind her back, like she's forcing herself to stay still as I walk toward her.

"I need my panties back."

I reach her and mirror her stance, placing my hands behind my back. I do it to stop myself from taking her as I truly wish to. "I'm afraid that isn't possible."

She tilts her head, but I notice the smile in her eyes. "Jared."

My name sounds perfect on her lips. "Layla." I draw out her name.

Her lip twitches.

Standing this close to her is torture. "Let me finish your tour of the garden. I think you may have been distracted earlier."

Her cheeks are pink, but I love the smile that grows on her face. I keep to my promise and show her the gardens that are set on twenty-two acres. Layla is more relaxed, and she takes in most of what I'm saying. Every once in a while, her gaze slips to my pocket, and I can tell she's thinking about her panties, which she isn't getting back.

We ended up back near the area where we had food and my first taste of her pussy. Everything has been cleared away, and I proceed to the house. It's been a while since we barely ate, and I'm sure William will have food ready for us.

Opening the front door for the first time, I feel relaxed. I disabled the camera system in the house. My father isn't here, and I want complete privacy with Layla.

She's quiet as we climb the stairs, and I want to know what's going on in her pretty head. She's looking around her, taking in all the pictures.

"Is that your father?" she asks as we continue to climb the stairs.

I don't have to look at which one she's referring to. His picture can't be missed by the sheer size of the photo that takes up residence on a large portion of the wall. "Yes."

"You don't talk about him."

I glance back and stop midstep.

Layla's eyes widen, and I see a flash of fear. I take her hand in mine and continue up the stairs. "What do you want to know?"

Her shoulders relax. "Do you have a good relationship with him?"

No.

"He's never hurt me." Physically. "He gives me everything I need," I answer honestly. I wouldn't have the life I have without him. He pulled me from the gutter. Yet there's an emptiness in this life that can't seem to be filled. I thought finding Layla would fill the void, but I don't feel whole.

"Emotionally?" Layla's question is low.

We reach the third floor, and I release her hand. Food is waiting for us in the living area. William has left two hotplates filled with food. I hold out my arm for Layla to go first. She steps up to the small table. I love the smell that emanates from her hair as I stand behind her.

"Are you hungry?"

She glances at me over her shoulder. "Yes."

I grin and pull out her chair. "You have worked up an appetite."

I love watching her get embarrassed. It's refreshing. I sit across from her and lift the lid off the plate. Steam and the aroma from the steak satisfy me.

Layla lifts her lid and smiles. "Wow, this looks amazing."

She starts to eat, and I watch her for a few moments until she notices and stops. "You never answered my question about your father."

I know.

I cut up a piece of steak. "No, not emotionally. He's a man." I grin and chew.

Layla's brows drag down. "Who do you talk to?"

"I'm okay, Layla." I want to erase the worry from her features.

She eats a few more bites of steak before she asks her next question. "What about your mother?"

These questions were to be expected. They shouldn't feel so hard. "Her name is Maura. She left when I was young." I hope my quick answer has Layla leaving it alone. I could ask her about sneaky Evelyn, who knew about me all along. I don't. I don't because Layla loves her, and she doesn't need another person to fucking disappoint her. And it doesn't matter anyway. She has me now, and she doesn't need Evelyn or Carl.

Layla thankfully directs the conversation to happier times. I'm laughing as we relive sledding down the hill at the back of our estate. We would steal empty coal bags, get inside them, and slide down the snow-covered hill at record speeds. The climb back up was just as fun, and when we got back to Bert and Ronnie's, we would be red from the cold, but inside, we would be warm from fun and laughter.

Time slips away, and I love this part—how easy it is with Layla. She's so animated when she speaks, and when she laughs, I want to smile.

"I'd better go soon." Layla sounds apologetic.

I check my phone. "It's only eight." What's the rush?

She shrugs. "I have a curfew at eleven."

I get out of my seat. "Curfew? You're nineteen." I reach for Layla and hold out my hand. She hesitates but takes my hand and stands up.

"I know, but they're protective."

A little too fucking much.

"I'll have you home by ten thirty." I cross my heart.

Layla laughs. "Why don't I believe you?"

I lean in, and her smile vanishes. I press my lips against hers. "I can call Evelyn and let her know you're spending the night."

Layla freezes. Desire darkens her blue eyes. She shakes her head. "I'd better stick to the curfew."

"I can't tempt you?" I press another kiss to her lips. This time, I'll let her go home, but it won't be for long. Soon, she'll be right beside me.

"Can I use your bathroom before I go?"

I reluctantly release her. "There's one in my bedroom."

She raises a brow.

I cross my heart again. "There is a bathroom in my bedroom."

She pivots toward my room but glances at me.

"You want me to show you?"

"I remember where your room is."

She leaves, and once she's gone, I take her panties out of my pocket. Holding them up to my nose, I inhale before stuffing them back into my pocket. I adjust my hard cock, which is bulges against my jeans.

The lights go out in the room. Evening light streams in front of the windows, casting shadows. I step out of the living room, and the hallway is also in darkness.

"Layla," I call and take a step toward my room.

The cock of a gun has me freezing. I turn slowly.

"You shouldn't have put your hands on me." Chester stands in the stream of light. His face is virtually unrecognizable from the beating I gave him. His left arm is in a sling, but he holds the gun steady in his right.

"What are you going to do? Shoot me?" I sneer.

He doesn't answer, and fear coils in my gut. "You think you can get away with it?" I ask him. "That no one saw you come in? My home has cameras everywhere."

"The cameras are off, Jared. Thanks to you."

How could he know that? My mind goes frantic. I hear the creak behind me, and Chester's head rises in that direction.

"My staff would have seen you." I step to the right, and his focus returns to me. He holds the gun higher.

"This is the gun you wanted me to get you. The serial number is erased. It's untraceable. Just like you wanted."

"Jared." Layla's voice is so close. A shiver steals the last of my warmth. The gun is no longer pointed at me. I turn as Layla frowns and steps closer.

"Go back!" I bark.

She looks at Chester with narrowed eyes, like she can't make him out. From her point of view, she wouldn't be able to.

"The lights went out." She's beside me now, and I grab her wrist, stopping her from going any further. She inhales sharply.

"The little bitch." Chester sounds gleeful. I'm ready to pull Layla behind me.

The explosion of the gun rips through the space, and warm blood coats my face.

CONTINUE THE DUET WITH SAVE ME (PART TWO OF THE BROKEN PEOPLE DUET)

START READING SAVE ME TODAY!

Sign up to my newsletter if you want to be notified about my new releases. HERE

About The Author

When Vi Carter isn't writing dark romance books, you can find her reading her favorite authors, baking, taking photos, or watching Netflix.

Married with three children, Vi divides her time between motherhood and all the other hats she wears as an Author.
Social Media Links for Vi Carter
Website
Facebook Reader Group
Facebook Author Page

ACKNOWLEDGEMENTS

I'm very lucky to have such amazing readers and Beta Readers. I want to thank the following people who worked with me on this book.

Developmental Editor: Amanda Cuff

Editor: Sherry Schafer

Proofreader: Michele Rolfe

Blurb was written by: Tami Thomason

Beta Readers

Amanda Sheridan

Laura Riley

Lucy Korth

Tami Thomason

Ashley Wheelock

Annas Book Nook

Other thanks:

Tom Korth

www.ingramcontent.com/pod-product-compliance
Lightning Source LLC
Chambersburg PA
CBHW030748190726
48285CB00003B/747